THE SECRET JEWISH SISTERS:

A WW2 Historical Novel, Based on the True Story of a Holocaust Survivor

BY TIKVA RAGER

Producer & International Distributor
eBookPro Publishing
www.ebook-pro.com

THE SECRET JEWISH SISTERS
Tikva Rager

Copyright © 2023 Tikva Rager

All rights reserved; no parts of this book may be reproduced or transmitted in any form or by any means, electronic or mechanical, including photocopying, recording, taping, or by any information retrieval system, without the permission, in writing, of the author.

Translation: Helene Hart
Contact: tikvar32@gmail.com

ISBN 9798323957378

Chapter 1

The train starts to move with a jarring screech of wheels. Huddled together, we look through the window and see Papa facing us and walking backward. He's holding a dripping umbrella in one hand, and waving to us and blowing kisses with the other. My sister, Suzy, just four years old, bursts into tears, and I, Rita, eight years old, try to comfort her and hide my tears.

"You remember that Papa promised to be waiting for us when we get to Belgium. He explained that he'll get there before us because he's driving there by motorcar with his friends, and they'll beat the train. And Mama may come with him if the doctor allows her to."

The day before our trip, I asked Papa, "Why did Mama go before us? Why's she not coming with us?" Before he answered, he looked and looked at me for so long, I noticed the black circles under his blue-gray eyes.

"You know that Mama's not that well, and she got a big fright when her best friends' husband was arrested and she was questioned by the police. That's why I suggested that she go on ahead to her cousin in Belgium. Just until I finish organizing our finances."

I remember that Mama's eyes were red from crying before she left us for Belgium. I miss her and I can't wait to see her waiting with Papa for us on the platform in Antwerp.

"And why aren't you coming with us?"

"Right now, it's not a good idea for the neighbors to think

we're leaving. As far as they know, you're just going to visit Mama. And it's not at all good for us to all be together."

I wanted to ask again why but something stopped me, as if I could feel inside that traveling together could be dangerous. Papa told me that if Suzy asks why he's coming on his own, I should tell her that he has to help his friends move their motorcar to Belgium, and only he knows the way. I felt like the older, responsible daughter. Papa added, "Suzy's more like Mama. She's sensitive, so perhaps it's better for her to not know that really, we have to leave Germany. As far as she's concerned, we're going to visit Mama."

We're both wearing blue dresses and our hair is in braids and tied with matching blue ribbons the same color as Suzy's eyes. We have a small suitcase with some sandwiches that Papa made last night and a book to read. If Suzy asks me to, I can read quietly to her.

Last night, when Suzy was already asleep, Papa told me how to behave on the train. "Try not to attract attention," he said. "And if there are any people in your car, it's best not to have a conversation with them. Simply answer politely if they address you. I'll take you onto the train and into your carriage, and I'll introduce you to the conductor. He's in charge of the train, and from time to time he'll come to check up on you and see how you are. I hope he'll keep to our agreement."

* * * *

Two elderly women enter the carriage. They're talking to each other, but every now and then they stare at us and I think they're whispering, "*Das sind jüdische mädchen.*" Those are Jewish girls...

I remember the first time I felt that bad days were coming. When my classmates, even my best friend, started to stay away from me and walked away from me and one of the rough street boys who everybody knew spat at me in the street.

"We aren't welcome here," Papa said when I told him about the boys.

The motion of the speeding train and the repetitive flat landscape rock me into a light sleep, and images of the last few days flood me. How on my way back from school, I saw a group of boys in brown uniforms beating a Jew with a beard and sidelocks. They made him kneel before them and sing, and they rolled with laughter. I was so afraid to go to school after that and I was worried about Papa; that I wouldn't find him at home when I got there. I can still hear the glass breaking in the Jewish stores. Life became scarier every day. And every day, the Jews were given new rules to live by. Boy, was I angry that I landed up being Jewish.

* * * *

Papa keeps his promise. He's waiting for us in Antwerp on the platform. Mama's not with him. Suzy and I jump on him, we're so happy, and the three of us dance around on the platform. Papa has tears in his eyes. People look at us in bewilderment, until someone approaches Papa, whispers something in his ear that sounds to me like the Yiddish that our grandparents used to speak to each other when they didn't want us to understand. Papa's face becomes serious and he stops showing how happy he is.

"Why didn't Mama come?"

"Mama's ill, she has pneumonia. She fell ill on the way to Antwerp. It was a difficult trip that took longer than planned. She couldn't stay with her cousin and was moved somewhere else." Without giving us more details, he adds, "I'm so glad that you arrived safely. Mama will join us when she gets better."

Papa hurries to hail a cab to the hotel we're going to be staying at for a few days. In the first few days, he leaves us on our own for a few hours while he looks for an apartment. He finds an apartment. It's a room and a half on the roof of a building in a very nice neighborhood. It has a doorman and a double bed, a wobbly table and some crates. Some of the crates are going to be our closet, and the rest are for sitting on. I think it's strange that the apartment is in such a beautiful place and the room's not furnished, but I can feel that I shouldn't ask too many questions. Suzy and I are going to be attending a Jewish school close to our apartment. It's called Yesod HaTorah, which Papa tells me means The Torah's Foundation in Hebrew, and my father's cousin, a very religious Jew, is the headmaster there. Papa's cousin asks him to observe the mitzvas. I know that at home in Germany he didn't observe them. Here at school in Antwerp, I do what the religious teachers teach me.

Papa has another cousin in Antwerp, and her husband is wealthy. He works with diamonds and he's also very observant and very religious.

"They observe all the mitzvas except for helping their relatives, stateless refugees like us. We're like a hump on their back to them," Papa says bitterly. "But humps without beards and sidelocks."

I eat lunch at the Jewish Agency's soup kitchen, and if I'm late I go hungry. Suzy eats at daycare. When we get home from school, our neighbors, a Belgian couple who don't have children of their own look after us until Papa comes home. Papa's finding it hard to find a job because he's a stateless refugee and he takes any work he can, no matter what. In the evenings, he's very tired and sad and praises me for learning Flemish so quickly.

After a week in daycare, Suzy starts yelling instead of talking like normal.

"Papa, could she have an ear infection? Do you think she can't hear well?"

"She's not complaining of pain, so it's not an ear infection."

"Suzy, tell me, why are you yelling so much?" I ask her.

"The kindergarten is for children who can't hear well because I talk to them and they don't answer me. They look at me only when I yell."

Papa's surprised and after a few moments he starts laughing and can't stop and I also start laughing. It takes Suzy two weeks to start chattering away in Flemish and she stops yelling. That's about the only time Papa's laughed since we've been in Antwerp.

At school they teach us about the Tisha B'Av fast because of the Temples being destroyed, and when Papa gets home in the evening and drops on the bed, he's so tired, I say to him, "Papa, it's Tisha B'Av today, you have to sit on the floor like me."

Papa's face turns so red with anger that I get a fright.

"As of tomorrow, I'm moving you from the Jewish school to a government school, even if I have to pay. Instead of taking proper care of the Jewish refugees from now, they're crying over what happened two thousand years ago."

* * * *

I really like my new school, even though it's a little far from our apartment, but I don't like being at our neighbors after school. I tell Papa that the man sits me on his lap and touches me all over my body and gives me horrible, wet kisses. Papa jumps up and runs next door and I can hear a big fight and Papa and the neighbor yelling. I peek out the door and see all the other neighbors gathering around and listening to the fight.

Red again with rage, Papa shouts, "You sick old man, is that what you do to little girls? How are you not ashamed of yourself?"

One of the neighbors tells Papa he should report him to the police.

The old man laughs in Papa's face and says, "You? You're going to go to the police? That's not a good idea—I'll tell them you're a Jewish refugee without documents who crossed the border illegally."

Papa musters all his courage and takes Suzy and me with him to the Belgian police to complain. The old man is called in for questioning. The police give Papa a few months to arrange the papers that will let us stay in Belgium. I don't ask what they did to the neighbor.

Papa finds another family for us to be with until he gets home from work in the evening.

After a few weeks of anxiously following the news, Papa comes home shaken and tells us, "The damned Germans have just occupied parts of Belgium, they'll be here soon."

Papa starts looking for a way to escape to Spain or England, but he doesn't have the money for it. Then he tries to send me and Suzy to Palestine through the Jewish Agency, but we can't go because we're too young. We stay in Belgium, which is now completely occupied, in our room and a half in the attic. Whenever I go out and come home, I run on the stairs because I'm so afraid of bumping into that disgusting old man.

Chapter 2

Summer is over and the leaves have all turned orange and red. I'm going to be nine soon. Someone bangs on the door and it's not even morning yet. It's still dark outside when I hear a man shouting in German, "*Raus zur arbeit!*" Out to work. I see Papa being shoved by two German police officers as he shouts to me, "Your coats, your coats, get yours and Suzy's and come with me. Don't stay here on your own."

Frightened and confused, I grab both our coats in one hand and Suzy's hand in the other, and I drag her with all my might after Papa. She's still half asleep. The street is very crowded. Everyone looks frightened and Suzy's crying and I'm shaking with fear. We stick close to Papa and he hugs us close. I hear him say, "They're all Jewish, they must be sending us east."

I don't remember how we got to the train station, maybe we walked there, all the time staying close to Papa in the dark. They push us onto the train that's waiting at the platform. Heavy doors slam shut and there's a strong, nasty smell in the crowded carriage. Everyone's sweating from fear. There's not enough air to breathe. We're locked in darkness. The train starts to shake and Papa's voice cracks with fury when he says, "It was that contemptible old man who betrayed us and informed them that we're Jewish refugees, without citizenship in any country."

I feel guilty. Maybe if I hadn't told Papa about the old man, we wouldn't have been caught. But I don't share this with Papa, I don't want to make him sad.

I don't know how long it is before the train leaves. Suddenly there's a loud deafening boom and the wheels screech. The train stops suddenly. Dad grabs Suzy and I fall and bash my leg hard, but I'm so scared of what's happening that I forget about the pain. There's a long threatening silence and then the doors open. I'm struck by the light, the cold air, and the smell of smoke. People who aren't German climb into the train and urge us out. They give us water and tell us to run, run toward the village houses that are close to the tracks. I remember the name of the village, Disenbeck. They blow up the locomotive and chunks of metal stain the green fields. Within a few minutes, everyone disappears and we're last. We stand there, it's a struggle to run with little Suzy and me with my injured leg. The big priest who gave us water before and showed everyone which way to run picks up Suzy and tells Papa to help me run after him to his sister's house. She doesn't have children of her own.

* * * *

Suzy and I are closed up in the house. We can't go out for fear of the Germans coming to look for anyone who escaped. Papa leaves us and goes with the priest. Three days later, the Germans arrive and go from house to house, and we all shake with fear. Paralyzing fear. In the middle of the night, Papa comes with the priest, who picks Suzy up while I hold Papa's hand and we walk for a long time in eerie silence. We're all breathing heavily except for Suzy, who's fallen asleep with her arms around the priest's neck. A car is waiting for us outside the village. It's headlights are covered in mud and we can barely see the road. Finally, the morning light breaks through the fog and we can see in the distance the blurred lines of a large building rising out of a hill, like the monastery in our city.

The priest pulls on the bell rope. A nun welcomes us and leads us to the Mother Superior, who motions to the nun who led us in to leave. She has a nice face, the Mother Superior, and she asks us in German what our names are. Papa hands her a bag, turns to us, and says, "There are documents and photos in the bag that the Mother Superior will keep for you," and adds, "I'm leaving you in good hands, I'll come to visit you as soon as I can."

He gets up quickly, thanks the Mother Superior, gives Suzy a hug, and then puts his arm around me and pulls me to the corner of the room. He has tears in his eyes and his mouth tremors when he says to me, "Don't forget that you're Jewish. The Mother Superior knows this but no one else can know. Not even your sister, because she's too young, and without meaning to, she may reveal that she's Jewish. I trust you, you're a very smart girl. I'll try to visit and bring you news from Mama. Take care of Suzy. I love you both. I'll be back, you'll see."

Papa leaves quickly and my sister runs after him and screams, "Papa, Papa."

The nun stops her with a hug and says, "He'll be back to get you after the war ends. Now, it's breakfast time, you must be hungry."

She rings the bell and a nun comes and leads us to a large hall with long tables where girls of all ages are sitting and eating in silence. The only sound is of cutlery clinking on the dishes and of Suzy's sobs, which are slowly dying down. The nun seats us at a table looking out at green fields, where war and pain have no place. I stroke Suzy's head, wipe away her tears with my bare hand, and whisper in German, "Oh, look, sausages! You love sausages."

I slice the sausages, stick my fork in a piece, pile some mashed potatoes on top, and hand her the fork. We finish the meal with hot tea. The nun who took care of us before leads us to another long hall. A dormitory with long neat rows of beds. Each bed has a small cabinet next to it. There's a uniform on my bed, a gray pinafore to wear over a brown dress, shoes, a big headscarf, and other bits and pieces, some of which I have to change because they don't fit me. Suzy's bed is in another hall. She'll come to collect us for lunch, the nun says, and adds that the Mother Superior said that afterward we are to bathe, rest, come for dinner at six o'clock, and then to prayers. I help Suzy bathe and dress. The water's freezing and she whines and doesn't make it any easier for me. She really is a spoiled little girl, but I love her so much. Utterly exhausted from the tough night, we collapse together in my bed. We wake up in a panic to see that the clock at the end of the hall shows a quarter to six.

After dinner, we're led to the prayer hall. I'm moved by the organ music and the singing of the girls' choir. They sound so good that it feels like they're washing away all the frightening events and suffering that I've been through recently. Now it's as if it was all just a bad dream. I'm dizzy from the sounds and from the bright colors in the windows and the images of white angels floating in the paintings. A calm comes over me and my eyes close. Suzy says it's so beautiful that she also wants to sing in the choir.

* * * *

For the first few days, Suzy and I are seated in the last row at church, and because we don't know the rules of the ceremony yet, we copy what the girls sitting in front of us do.

We want to be like everyone else, but we still speak German to each other.

The first night, after the lights are put out, I can't fall asleep because of Suzy's crying. She doesn't want to sleep away from me in the younger girls' dormitory. The nun in charge stops her by force from coming to my dormitory. I hear the slap that Suzy gets, which only makes her scream more and cry for help in German. "I want Rita, I want my sister!"

The helpless nun asks the Mother Superior for help, and the Mother Superior decides that until she gets used to it, for the first few nights I can sit with Suzy until she falls asleep. This arrangement goes against the strict rules of the convent. The girls my age say that they're giving in to her more than to the others, and I explain that she's the youngest and she's also the only one who has a sister. After lights out, I get into her bed and we whisper and tell each other all about what happened that day and we both say how much we miss Mama and Papa, until Suzy falls asleep and until she gets used to her new life.

"Rita, it's true that Mama was really pretty, Papa always said so, right? Sometimes I can't really remember what she looked like."

"Yes Suzy, she's blonde with blue eyes and you look like her. I look more like Papa, and I have gray eyes."

"Yes, but you're also beautiful, even if Papa wasn't that handsome."

I give her a hug. She's so good and kind, just like the nuns want us to be.

* * * *

I've become like both her mother and her father and I'm only nine myself, not even four years older than her.

In the cold mornings of the first winter, Suzy has trouble waking up. I wake her up as gently as Mama used to, when things were still good. One morning, when her pretty face still looks sleepy, she says to me, "Last night I saw Mama in a dream, but her face was fuzzy and when I tried to get closer to her, I thought her face looked like the face in that painting of Saint Mary in the church."

Then she adds with a smile, "I think maybe I have two mothers. Actually, I even have three mothers, because you wake me up in the morning like Mama used to. Does this happen to you too?"

I can't breathe for a moment and I don't answer.

Will I also forget what Mama looks like? In the short prayers that morning, I talk to Saint Mary and ask her to please take care of Papa and Mama, so that they can come back quickly.

I never saw Papa praying at home, but Mama would light candles on Friday evening and on the Jewish holidays Papa and I would go to the synagogue because Mama insisted, which was strange because she never went to synagogue herself. I would stay in the yard to play with other girls who didn't go inside. One time, Papa took me inside to where they pray. Papa said Yom Kippur is a special day for Jews. I was six years old but they still wouldn't let me be with Papa. I could barely find him from the balcony above, he was all wrapped up in white clothes like everyone else. They were all rocking their bodies and making such a loud noise, as if they were trying to break through the ceiling.

"Papa, what did the people say?"
"They asked God to forgive them for the bad deeds they did."
"Have you also done bad deeds?"
"Yes, sometimes we don't even notice when we hurt others."
"And does God forgive them?"
"They all hope so."

Chapter 3

Winter is coming so fast. The dormitory is freezing in the morning, I can feel it in my bones, and in the dim light it's hard to make out the girls who are starting to wake up. My body's begging for another moment in bed, to pamper myself with a good stretch, but in my battle with the strict morning duties, it's clear who the winner is. Every second comes with a defined task: Sleep on your back with your arms crossed, dress modestly without exposing any of your body parts unnecessarily, stand in line for the bathroom, brush your teeth, wash your face with cold water, don't linger. Make your bed and kneel beside it to say a short morning prayer. We stand in line in silence before we file into the dining hall. Suzy arrives at the last minute. I see her at the end of the line and I feel relieved. If we fail to stick to the strict schedule, our deviation is corrected through punishment. That sometimes means having our knuckles rapped or being hit somewhere else, and a prayer asking for forgiveness and promising to do better.

The tension that was in the air begins to disappear with the morning light and after a filling meal. I'm happy we have school lessons for three hours. The convent is mostly a school for girls from good families who pay to live at the boarding school, but it also accepts poor and homeless girls and the local farmers' daughters who go home every day. Lessons are basic and also include a lot of religious stories about saints and miracles, and preaching about helping others and humility. Most of the nun-teachers are kind and they praise me for being a good student who helps my friends who have trouble with math.

I'm the nun-teacher's favorite, and one day she asks me to go to the library to pick up a book that she left on the table and forgot to bring with. A long dark corridor leads to the library with picture after picture of saints covering the walls and freezing cold flowing from the corners. A heavy smell of books in leather covers welcomes me. It's a smell I recognize, but for a few moments I don't know where from. Suddenly, I see Papa sitting in a fancy leather armchair in Opa's library in his home, where we lived. He's hunched over a book and his reading glasses are balanced on his nose.

"Go call Papa for dinner, everyone's already waiting," Mama sent me to get him while Opa grumbled under his thick mustache about the bad manners of the *Ostjuden*. That's what he called the Jews from Eastern Europe...the eastern Jews...and he didn't mean it nicely. There was no love lost between Opa, who was a wealthy man, and my educated father from Poland who snatched up his wonderful daughter. The image in my mind of Papa in the library is fuzzy, it's been so long since we parted that some of his image has been erased. I sob but quietly, and tears pour from my eyes, either from longing or from anger at myself for hardly ever thinking about him anymore, or maybe it's for both reasons. I give myself a few minutes until my tears dry. The teacher notices something and I can see that her eyes look confused. During our midday break I tell Suzy about what happened. She doesn't even remember that we had a library.

* * * *

Suzy loves the activities we have after we have a short rest in the middle of the day.

"Today I knitted a scarf, it's a bit like Mama's scarf, and blue, like her eyes," Suzy tells me enthusiastically. "What did you do, Rita?"

"I learned to darn socks and change the elastic thread in our pants."

The craft room is full of light that pours in through the tall windows. Looking through the windows and as far as we can see, there are fields that are green in the summer and covered with snow in the winter. We can see the farmers on their full carts bringing their produce to the convent. They bring sacks of potatoes, crates of grapes. (I can smell their delightful aroma even now.) They also bring us pork meat, eggs, milk, and cheese. But less and less as the war goes on. Still, the small farm at the convent improves our situation.

Our time in the craft room is relaxing. We learn to sew, knit, mend clothes, and embroider. And we chat with each other during the activities and make friends. The nuns read wondrous stories about acts of kindness, about being content with a little, and about helping others. Everyone likes Suzy, and she makes friends with Klara, whose mother is with the angels and her father remarried and put her education in the hands of the nuns for a fee.

"Rita, look what Klara gave me, and you too—pictures of Mother Mary. They all hang them above their beds. During the break, we'll hang them up."

"Okay," I answer in a choked voice.

Armed with a hammer and nails, Suzy climbs onto her bed and I direct her to the exact point above the center of the bed. She manages to bang the nail in and hangs up the picture of Mother Mary. She climbs down and crosses herself. When we hang mine over my bed, she hits her thumb nail with the hammer. It must hurt her a lot but Suzy surprises me and doesn't give up. She finishes the job even though her nail is turning blue. Then she winces in pain.

"Oh Suzy, you need to make it cold, like Mama would. It helps."

"Rita, it really hurts, but Jesus suffered much more when the evil Jews crucified him."

"Who told you it was the Jews?"

"Klara's father told her."

"I'll go get some ice to ease the pain." On the way I tell myself that I'll ask the teacher if it's true what Klara's father said, but even if it is true, it still doesn't mean that all Jews are bad.

* * * *

The last hours of the day after relaxing in the craft room and before dinner, we have hours of chores such as carrying buckets of water, cleaning the livestock's pens, tending to the vegetable garden, and especially kitchen work, which was mostly peeling piles and piles and piles of potatoes. Doing the peeling hurts Suzy's small, unskilled hands. The head cook, a crude peasant woman, reprimands Suzy because she peeled off a lot of potato flesh with the peel. Suzy tries but she just can't do better. As punishment, the cook tells her that she'll cook all the peels she peeled and that's what she'll have for her dinner until she learns to peel properly. Suzy's meal is the big pile of skins instead of regular potatoes. Although there's less room left for the other parts of the meal, she does get a fair amount of potato flesh after she peels off the peel. I suggest to her to make even thicker peels next time. That way, I can also enjoy a few chunks. When the cook notices she's furious and drags us both to the Mother Superior and complains about us. The Mother Superior asks us to explain our actions. Suzy defends herself while whimpering and holding out her raw hands, and she says that she tried to peel properly but she just couldn't work out how to.

I stand next to her and say, "I'm the one who deserves punishment because I told Suzy to make the peels as thick as she could."

The Mother Superior can't hide the smile on her face and tells the cook that we'll be punished.

And from then until Suzy is a little older, she's released from peeling and our potato portions go back to their normal size. I'm punished with kitchen duty for a week during the midday break and prayers.

* * * *

This is our third year at the convent. We're busy making Christmas decorations. The craft room is packed full of colorful paper decorations, bright drawings and pictures, the sound of stage props being sawed, and we joyful girls preparing for the holiday while waiting to hear the role we'll get in the traditional nativity play. The teacher chooses me to play Mary, the mother of the newborn Christ. I get butterflies in my stomach, and all around me the girls are disappointed and a little jealous that they weren't chosen for the coveted role.

That evening, after prayers, I stay behind in the hall so I can be alone for a little. I kneel before the image of the Madonna and place my hand over my mouth as tears stream down my face. The Mother Superior, who as usual is doing her nightly inspections, hears me crying, comes to me, and places her hand on my shoulder. She asks me why I'm crying.

Sobbing, I answer, "I'm asking for forgiveness from the Madonna for playing Saint Mary on Christmas Eve and for being Jewish."

The Mother Superior caresses my tearstained face, and says, "Rita, it's all right, you're allowed to play Saint Mary. After all, both Mary and Jesus were Jews, and now my child, pray and go to bed, it's already late."

Emotional after the hearing the Mother Superior's words, I toss and turn in my sleep. Papa appears in my dream and I tell him that Jesus and the Holy Madonna were Jews and that I'm asking them to make the war end quickly and for him and Mama to return safely and that I'm still keeping the secret he asked me to. Papa's image becomes blurred and looks like one of the paintings of the saints that Suzy always says looks like our father.

Sometimes I get angry at Papa for making me hide such a huge secret from Suzy. Dad warned me not to tell her or anyone else. I'm doubly troubled for having to keep such a big secret to myself while at the same time hiding the truth from Suzy about herself. I'm afraid of her reaction if I do tell her, and at the same time I'm doing as he asked. I understand that revealing the truth could be dangerous to us both, maybe even to the Mother Superior. Sometimes I wonder why Papa didn't just keep it from me like he did from Suzy. Startled by my anger, I immediately ask Mother Mary to forgive me.

Papa left me a heavy burden to carry. I have no way to unload it. Only once I told Katie, my best friend in the convent, that after the war I would tell her a big secret, and although she pleaded with me to tell her now, I didn't. Papa's orders and my survival instinct are that strong.

* * * *

We're isolated and far from the nearest city, which means the German soldiers from the garrison in the city come less often. When they do come, the Mother Superior softens them up with the wine that the nuns make in the small winery in the convent's cellar. Every month, she travels to the German headquarters in a wagon filled with boxes of wine that in the good days they would sell to the farmers of the area. In wartime, meeting with the Germans is part of maintaining good relations with them, and they're always happy to have the wine and a chat in German with the wise Mother Superior

A long time passes before I dare to ask the nun-teacher, whom I love, where the Mother Superior's good German comes from. She looks at me for a long time, hesitating whether to answer my question, which is not appropriate for a student.

Nevertheless, she answers, "The Mother Superior is German, like you. She was orphaned as a child and grew up in a convent, joined the order of nuns and ten years ago, much to our luck, she was promoted and became the Mother Superior of our convent."

Chapter 4

Winter is in full swing. The fields surrounding the convent are covered in snow and blend with the white clouds in the sky. We're busy preparing for Christmas in the craft room. We're making and decorating Christmas cards. Each girl must prepare cards for three friends. We chose the friends beforehand from a list that the nun in charge is keeping to make sure we all receive Christmas cards. Each card will come with a chocolate, which we can choose from a selection of shapes. Some are shaped like angels, and there are stars, tiny dolls, hearts, and bells. They'll be waiting under our pillows when we return from Christmas Mass.

I look up for a moment to see Suzy engrossed in coloring in one of the cards she's making. I try to catch her attention and smile at her. I want to tell her about the dream I had. Papa was in it and I told him what the Mother Superior told me, that Jesus and Saint Mary were also Jews. But I stop before she sees me. After all, she doesn't know that she's Jewish. The words of the Mother Superior calmed me down but also confused me. Is it possible to be Jewish and pray to Mother Mary and believe in Jesus? Why don't the peasant women who work in the convent like the Jews? Don't they know that Jesus was Jewish? And he, after all, wanted to help people who were also Jewish. Am I Jewish then, or Christian? Can people choose what they want to be? Can a person be both at the same time?

"Everyone who's participating in the nativity play, please come to the rehearsal."

The call to rehearsal interrupts my thoughts. I do my best to do as the nun tells me for my role as the mother of Jesus. I've memorized the words of the song that I'll be singing to Baby Jesus when he grows up.

* * * *

There are so many preparations leading up to Christmas day. Our hands swell and turn red from all the cleaning. Every day we have to shovel the snow that's piled up on the steps and paths leading to the church so that the farmers from around will be able to come to celebrate with us.

Christmas Eve, which we've been preparing for the past month for, is finally here. The morning starts as usual with school lessons, but not as usual, the teacher tells us about the many miracles that Jesus Christ performed. I already know about some of them. I especially like the miracles he did to heal the sick and restore eyesight to the blind and feed poor and hungry people. Maybe I'll learn to be a nurse because I'm happy to work in the convent's infirmary.

Our lunch is smaller than usual because we have a festive and especially delicious meal waiting for us that evening. And the midday break is longer than usual because the holiday ceremony starts at midnight because of Midnight Mass. During the afternoon break, we each find a smart outfit on our beds, which we'll be wearing at the meal and for Mass. The clothes for Mass are kept from year to year, long, white robes with braided belts that tie at the waist and hang down almost to our knees. The belts are in a variety of colors and we can choose any color we want. Some of the girls argue because they all want red. I also like the color red and suddenly I remember the red dress that was made specially for me for my last birthday before we left Germany, it was such a beautiful party. The memory makes me sad and I no longer care what color belt I get. The girls from the choir are wearing garlands made from fabric flowers on their heads. It's Suzy's first year performing with the choir, and she chooses a light blue belt and garland the same color as her eyes. She's so sweet and happy, and she's also going to sing a short solo, which she's been practicing for a few nights in her squeaky voice.

Tonight, we're exempt from setting the tables so that our robes remain clean for next year, and we have to take great care during the meal. The peasant women set the tables and they'll be serving the food. The festive meal is very late and I'm ravenous and also excited over the role I'll be playing in the play. Tonight, the nuns are dining with us but at a separate table. The Mother Superior is seated at one end of the table, and the convent's priest, who's also the village's priest, is seated at the other. The hall glows from the white tablecloths, the bright white robes, the candles, and the many, many flowers. The red flames of the lit candles around the hall wave every time a person passes by them, and their silhouettes spread along the walls as if they're tiny angels who've come to celebrate the holy day with us. The Christmas tree is lit with colorful lamps and decorated with the decorations we made ourselves. The aromas of the dishes make me giddy. The Mother Superior says grace and blesses us, we drink a little of the wine, the priest makes a short sermon. I can't follow his sermon.

How delicious the food is! We each get a little bit of many dishes. The meat is tender and melts in our mouths, and we even have the pickled asparagus that we picked at the beginning of last spring when the snow started to melt. How hard it is to pick asparagus! You have to pick it from the base that's still in the half-frozen earth, and be careful not to break the long and delicate stem. Our shoes get wet and our toes freeze.

    The ringing of the bells at midnight makes the air tremor with great force, as if the sky is about to split open. For a moment we freeze in place. Quietly and reverently, we follow the Mother Superior to church, and on our way, we see the lines of farmers and their families who are also making their way to the church. They're dressed in their Sunday best. The women are wearing smart but busy hats that have waited all year for the big celebration. The boys are in suits that have been passed down from child to child, and the men are in suits that for the most part haven't grown at the right pace for their owners. Just like them, some of our robes don't fit our bodies well, but the atmosphere is festive. People wish each other a Merry Christmas, either with a handshake or with a nod of the head from afar, and they fill the church pews on both sides of the aisle. At the center of the stage, there's a marble baby Jesus as naked as the day he was born. The last to enter are the clergy, who walk around the stage. They're led by the altar boy who's carrying the incense thurible, and when he moves it, incense disperses like a white cloud and its smell fills the church. The priest gives a sermon, which is interrupted from time to time by calls of "Amen," and I wait to be called up to the stage, which is now screened off from the audience.

    It's time. The curtain opens and I'm already on the stage, sitting on the straw in the stable where Jesus was born. Two white angels float toward me, touch me gently, and tell me that I will give birth to Jesus Christ our Savior. As they enter and exit the stage, they're accompanied by beautiful singing. I lean toward the crib beside me, in which beautiful little white marble Jesus is lying. I sing him a lullaby with the choir accompanying me. It seems to me that, like in the pictures, Baby Jesus is stretching his little hands out to me. I love him so much, and my eyes fill with tears. The choir sing along with the organ, "*Stille Nacht, Heilige Nacht.*" (Silent Night. Holy Night.) What a wonderful melody, it penetrates my soul and my heart almost explodes with pleasure. It feels like God's spirit is hovering around me and I surrender to the intoxicating feeling.

Chapter 5

Spring is in the air. The melting snow reveals green fields and paths, and all that remains of it are piles on the side, icy snow that's hardened. Streams of water wash over the world as if trying to wash away the cold of the long winter, the cold that keeps us shut indoors through the winter. In the spring and summer, after Holiday and Sunday Mass, we're allowed to go out into the yard to play and walk in the fresh air as long as we don't wander too far from the convent grounds.

I don't like to join the girls on their walks because they're always asking for details about their friends' pasts, and I, of course, have something to hide. I have one good friend, Katie, who has difficulty walking, and I don't tell even her that I'm Jewish.

"You and your books! Your eyes are already red and tired from reading so much," Suzy protests. Using her special charm, she closes my book and pulls me by my hand.

"Come, everyone's outside. It's good for the body and it'll make you happy inside."

Carried away by her lovable vitality, I ask, "And what are you planning for me?"

"Klara's going to show us a skipping game with a rope that she learned from the peasant women when she went to visit her father on the weekend. She brought back a rope. Two girls hold it, one at each end, and they spin it round and round. And one at a time, the girls take turns and have to jump and skip over it when it reaches the ground without touching it."

"Oh, really, Suzy, you're as light as a feather. It's not for me, and how will you all manage with your long dresses?"

"We can lift the hem up a little, we'll try."

"That's a sight I'd like to see," I answer and sit down heavily on the bench on the side of the yard. From there I can watch her and her friends jumping in turn. The girls who succeed continue, and those who fail replace the girls swinging the rope.

I look at the girls playing. They cram into a line and wait for their turn. We're all dressed in the same brown uniforms with gray pinafores and white collars. They remind me of a colony of penguins that I saw this week in a lesson on animals. They stand in perfect order, so similar to each other. But when the girls jump, each one is different. Nora, who's a big, heavy girl, pulls gingerly on her dress and purses her lips. She jumps out of time with the spinning rope and steps heavily on it, failing. She accepts the verdict and takes the place of one of the girls spinning the rope. Anna is next. She's so tall, and she tries to lower her head without success. She runs into the rope and gets hit on her head. She leaves the game. She doesn't want to play anymore. Suzy pulls her dress up with the greatest of ease to reveal her brown stockings and slender legs and skips like a doe. Her cheeks are flushed and her eyes are glowing with pleasure. Although I want to, I don't dare to join the game.

Why am I so heavy and don't know how to be happy like Suzy? Am I jealous of her? Oh no, it's a sin to be jealous, I think, angry with myself. Jealousy's forbidden, and I love her so much. She's mine and so different from me. All her friends like her, and she has absolute faith in Mother Mary, in good Jesus, and she has me as an older and loving sister. I ask God to forgive me. I again start worrying about how she'll react when Papa returns and she finds out that she's Jewish. All she knows about the Jews is that they betrayed Jesus, and she, as a Christian, is better than they are. The truth is, even I don't know what it is to be Jewish. I just keep hearing that they're bad, and I don't think that I'm bad. Can Papa feel how hard it is for me to keep my promise to remember who I am? Does he know how hard it'll be for Suzy when she eventually learns what we've been hiding from her? Oh Papa, where are you? When will you come to see us? I want to talk to you so much. Have you been caught up by the war?

An argument breaks out and interrupts my thoughts, and I quickly hide my damp eyes.

"You touched the rope, you lost, and now you have to spin it."

"That's not true, I didn't touch it, you're imagining it," the girl who's turn it is to jump retorts. The argument grows fiercer and other girls get involved, taking sides.

"You did touch it," Suzy says angrily.

"Rita, you were sitting on the side, what did you see?" Suzy's friend, Klara, turns to me.

"It's not fair!" The girl who's refusing to admit she failed gets angry at me. "You can't judge because you're Suzy's sister."

Chapter 6

Like on every winter morning, today too, we're standing shivering from cold in the classroom. Our hands are frozen and we're waiting for the nun-teacher to arrive. It's a normal school day, but we're in for a surprise. Together with the teacher, the Mother Superior enters the classroom, a kind smile on her face. It's not that she never smiles, not at all, but her smile today is different. It's as if today she has something happy to tell us. She looks at us as if she knows what we're thinking, because she's very wise. The girls in the class are a little afraid of her. Suzy told me what the girls say—with a hint of jealousy—that she gives me preferable treatment. That's because she gave me the part of Mother Mary in the nativity play, and she always calls me to help her with important jobs. It's true, she does smile at me whenever she sees me, maybe because I'm a very good student and I help the girls who have a hard time with their studies.

She motions for us to sit down and says, "This year, you are starting to prepare for your Holy Communion. It will take place at the end of the year, because then you will all be twelve years old and mature enough to consent and want to bear the burden of the church. Once a week, the priest will give you a lesson in which you will learn chapters of the New Testament and the principles of the Christian religion. You will also be summoned for your first confession before the priest. Leading up to the communion, I will call you in one at a time and discuss how you're progressing in your studies and your willingness to join the Catholic community."

The Mother Superior finishes speaking and leaves the classroom, and I'm left utterly confused. I know that babies from Christian families are baptized when they're born, and I thought that a baby who's baptized is already Christian. That means that I'm not Christian because I haven't been baptized. Papa even told me before we said goodbye that he arranged false papers for me and Suzy that he gave to the convent. The papers say we were baptized.

Suddenly I remember him saying to me, "Your real papers are hidden somewhere, and only the Mother Superior knows about it."

All day I walk around asking myself, Why do you have to take communion to become a Christian? Why are the other girls already considered Christians before going through the sacrament?

I don't dare to ask the teacher but the question keeps nagging at me so much that in one of the priest's classes, I ask why we need the rite of communion if a person who's been baptized is already Christian.

The priest contemplates his words before answering, "We are not born Christians, we must become one. The Sacrament of Baptism is performed when we're born, it's not performed of our own free will. It's the will of our parents who raise us as Christians. According to Jesus, baptism is the release of a person from original sin. Baptism purifies the body and soul, it's like being reborn with a pure and clean soul. It enables eternal life in Heaven. Later on, the Rite of Communion is about voluntary acceptance, not coercion, so you learn about the New Testament and pass a test. Baptism is a necessary condition for this."

I'm not sure what he means by original sin. Is it that they didn't obey God? Or could it be that they simply didn't think enough and were easily tempted by the snake to eat from the tree of knowledge of good and evil? Suzy says I always have too many questions.

"That's true, I do," I answer Suzy. "It's because I really like the stories of the New Testament and Jesus, who loved children and everyone so much and only wanted to do good for people when he saw how much evil there was in the world. And I don't understand why the Jews of that time didn't understand that he was the Messiah. If I'd been alive in those days, I would surely have followed him."

I couldn't share with her the new worry that was gnawing at me, about how I would go through the Rite of Communion if I was never baptized.

After a few months of studying in preparation for the Holy Communion, it's my turn to talk to the Mother Superior.

"The priest told me that you're an excellent student in religious studies. But you know that no one can force you to accept Christianity. You have to want to."

Excitedly, I tell her, "I believe in Jesus, I love Mother Mary, and I don't want to be a Jew anymore. It's not good for me to be Jewish, even if Papa told me not to forget that I am. Jesus was born Jewish and so was I. You are all protecting me from the Nazi Germans, and I want to be with you. I love praying in church, I love the Saints and all the holidays, Christmas, Easter. Help me to be a Christian."

"I want to help, but we have two problems. You need to be baptized without anyone knowing other than me and the priest, of course. Not even your sister Suzy can know so that no one finds out that you're Jewish. I also need your father's consent."

I wipe the tears from my eyes. "But I don't know where Papa is, I haven't heard from him or seen him in three years."

I drink the water she hands me and she replies, "I have something to tell you that'll surprise you. It's good news. The priest has a way to contact your father and he'll find out what he thinks."

"What!!" I give a muffled scream. "The priest knows where he is and how he is, and I didn't know. Why wasn't I told?"

"Don't forget that we're at war. In a few days, the priest will let you know your father's decision."

My heart skips a few beats. I'm trembling all over when I leave the Mother Superior's room. During evening prayers, I ask Saint Mary to help me become a true Christian.

I can't fall asleep at night. Thoughts are racing through my head. And what if Papa doesn't consent? And what is the relationship between him and our priest? What are they hiding from me?

"Why have you got dark circles around your eyes? You've had them for days," Suzy asks me. I see the concern in her eyes.

I don't answer and I rush to the priest's lesson, hoping for an answer from Papa.

A few days later, the priest leans over to me during class and whispers, "Your father gave his consent, and he'll come in secret for the baptism ceremony."

Chapter 7

On my way to class today I tripped twice because I'm so distracted by the thousand questions making my head explode. I'm so happy that Papa has agreed to my baptism, but how is it possible that he approves and is coming to the ceremony if he asked me not to forget that I'm Jewish? How does he even know about the ceremony? Why, after we haven't heard from him or seen him for so long, can he suddenly attend the ceremony? Should I tell Suzy? If Suzy finds out that I'm going to be baptized, then she'll also find out that we're Jewish. It'll be like a bomb's been dropped on her head. Well, then, I won't tell her. Am I allowed not to tell her? He is, after all, her father too, and she hasn't seen him for so long. Maybe Papa has his reasons for allowing it? Maybe he knows that if they don't baptize me, I won't be able to receive Holy Communion, and then everyone will know that I'm Jewish, and Suzy too. Maybe it's because he's concerned for our safety, and it's a very, very wise decision. Mama always said that Papa was terribly learned and smart, and that's why she fell in love with him.

Oh, how I miss him, I want to see him so badly, and maybe they can bring Mama with. He'll be able to answer all my questions, that's for sure.

* * * *

I don't tell Suzy.

One Sunday after morning prayers, Suzy's class is sent on a field trip. The Mother Superior signals to me to stay in the church. The main doors close and the priest and Papa enter through a back door. I can barely recognize him. My breath catches, I can't speak. Half his gaunt face is covered by a black hat like the peasants wear. His cheeks are sunken and his eyes are red. The rough clothes he's wearing are hanging on him, and he looks almost like a child in fancy dress. He runs to me. I fall into his arms and he hugs me tight. I burst out crying and can't stop, releasing more than three years of tension, three years of wanting to keep my promise to him without wanting to be Jewish. I believe in Jesus. I love Mother Mary and I pray to her. It's been three years of hiding from my sister who we really are and wanting to be like everyone else. Papa cries with me.

He strokes my wet face and says, "When I left, you were a child, and now you're already a young lady. We were robbed of three years of being together."

The Mother Superior urges us to rush, Papa can't stay long because it's a free Sunday and Suzy will be coming back soon from the trip and looking for me. We need to leave a little time to spend together.

We have an emergency baptism. First, the priest places his hand on my head and recites a prayer and a blessing. I feel drops of holy water dripping on my head and the oil on my forehead that he uses to anoint me. It feels like the water and oil are penetrating my body and purifying me. And the ceremony is over. The Mother Superior and the priest leave me and Papa alone and wait outside. In the short time we've been given, I ask about Mama. Papa takes both my hands in his and I can feel how hard it is for him to answer.

"Mama was sick, she caught pneumonia. Her trip from Germany to Belgium was difficult and took a long time in harsh and cold conditions. She's finding it hard to recover. I'm very worried about her. Unfortunately, I can visit her very rarely because it puts us both in danger. She's very lonely and despondent. The last time I saw her, she thought I was her father who'd come to visit her."

"But she'll get better in the end. I'll pray to Mother Mary," I answer, but my stomach turns with worry.

I can feel that he's not telling me the whole harsh truth about Mama, and when I ask if she's missing Suzy and me, he doesn't reply. He changes the subject and asks about Suzy. I answer that she's happy, that she has lots of friends, she joined the choir, she loves the church and feels that she belongs to it, and suddenly the question that I was afraid to ask bursts out of me. "Papa, why? I don't understand. It was so difficult to do as you asked, to not forget that I'm Jewish. So why have you agreed now to have me baptized? I prayed to Mother Mary that you'd agree. Did my prayer reach you?"

Papa caresses my head and answers, "The priest is the one who asked for my consent. We're working together, and it has to be a secret. I know how difficult it is for you and that you don't want to be Jewish. I'm releasing you from my request to make it easier for you and to allow you to believe in what you feel. But the main reason that I consented is to protect you and Suzy until the war ends. I'm not converting to Christianity. I don't believe in God or in his messenger Jesus. You can always decide who you want to be when the danger passes, but until then, even though you want to be and you feel Christian, don't reveal your background."

Dad stands up, hugs me tightly, and adds, "I'll try to come to your Holy Communion, and to see Suzy as well. I love you both."

Papa and the priest climb onto the bicycles that are waiting for them in the back yard, wave goodbye, and through the tears in my eyes, I watch them ride away into the distance until they're just two black dots that disappear on the horizon of green fields.

"Your father will attend the Holy Communion. Now go wash your face and rest until dinner." The Mother Superior strokes my head, which only makes me cry harder.

"I'm happy that Papa came, but I'm also sad because now I have to hide from Suzy that I saw him, and worry about what'll happen if she doesn't recognize him when he visits again. It's been three years since she saw him, and she was only five years old."

"You're right. Maybe you should prepare her before they meet again," the Mother Superior answers. "I'll call you tomorrow for a talk. You remember, I have a talk with each of the girls before the ceremony. You can tell her after our talk that I told you that your father will be attending the ceremony."

After my baptism and seeing Papa, I can't fall asleep for days. I think he's hiding the truth about Mama from me. It's been so long since she got sick, how is it possible that she still hasn't recovered? I'm terrified by the thought that she could be dead and he doesn't want to tell me so that he won't dampen my happiness over the Holy Communion. I try to push away the bad thoughts I have before going to sleep. I pray that I'll be able to answer all the questions that the priest is going to ask about the Christian faith. We've been studying for this all year and I want to excel.

Chapter 8

I return from my talk with the Mother Superior and rush off to see Suzy. Enthusiastically, I go into every detail of our talk, just to put off telling her about Papa.

"The Mother Superior asked me if I'm willing to bear all the duties of Christianity, such as not sinning, understanding why I sinned, confessing my sins, and performing the punishments that the priest will impose on me, attending Sunday Mass at church, when the priest gives the worshipers wine and bread that become the blood and flesh of Jesus, because this is what Jesus told his disciples to do," I go on and on. "I told her excitedly that I'm willing to bear all the duties. 'If so,' the Mother Superior said. 'If you're doing this from your own free will, then after the ceremony, you'll begin to live a truly Christian life. You'll be able to distinguish between good and evil. You'll be filled by the Holy Spirit, which will give you the strength to face all of life's difficulties.' At the end of the meeting, she asked me again if I understood and was willing to accept the duties of Christianity."

Suzy hugs me and says, "I'm sure you'll be an even better Christian than you already are."

"I'm going to try very hard. And now I have something wonderful to tell you that the Mother Superior told me at the end of the meeting. At first, I couldn't believe what I was hearing. Papa's coming to my Holy Communion!"

Suzy's face turns pale, her blue eyes widen in astonishment, and she doesn't utter a word. She finally lets out a deep sigh and says, "What? How can that be? How does he know about it?"

"What's wrong, Suzy, aren't you happy?"

"Of course, I'm happy that Papa's going to come and that nothing bad has happened to him during the war. But I don't know if I'll recognize him after so long."

I hug her and say, "It's impossible not to recognize Papa."

* * * *

The Sunday of our celebration is here. The ringing of the church bells sounds even more wonderful to me than usual. The relatives of the girls receiving Holy Communion fill the first rows, which have been reserved for them. The church is lit with lights and candles, which are everywhere. The ceremony is beginning soon, and I'm waiting with the other girls to begin. I don't see Suzy waiting outside for Papa.

The ceremony begins.

The choir, accompanied by the organ, sound like the angels I so love. The priest walks down the carpet that's been spread from the entrance to the stage and the altar. He's dressed in a very ornate red robe, and the sleeves of the white garment underneath are sticking out from under it. He has a tall white bonnet on his head, and its golden trim comes down over his shoulders. After him, the communion girls walk in wearing white dresses that reach just below the knee and floral garlands on their heads. They're holding lit candles. I'm first in line after the priest, and in both hands, I'm holding the silver bowl in which the sacramental bread has been placed. We line up on stage facing the guests.

The priest recites a short prayer and I anxiously look for Papa and Suzy in the crowd. I breathe a sigh of relief when I see him holding Suzy's hand as she proudly leads him to the front row, where the families are sitting. This time Dad is wearing a new suit, his shoes are shiny, his face is cleanshaven, and when he removes his stylish hat, I see that his hair is neat. It's my old Papa. I see him turn to Suzy and point to me, and I guess he's asking why my dress is long, unlike the other girls' dresses. I see the pride in his face when Suzy explains loudly that I'm the best student in religious studies.

The priest stands with the guests on one side and the row of girls on the other. I walk toward him and my hands tremble as I hand him the bowl of sacramental bread. He places the bowl on the stand next to him, places his hand on my head, anoints my forehead with the holy oil, and places a piece of the sacramental bread on my tongue after I taste the wine. He blesses me with a special prayer, while the choir sings in the background. My head is spinning, It's like I'm floating above the choir of angels, and I'm an angel too. One by one the girls approach the priest and each one receives a blessing and tastes the holy wine and sacramental bread. The ceremony ends with a short prayer. At the end, the whole congregation stands up as they say Amen with a penetrating force that shakes my soul.

Holy Communion is over.

We each receive a copy of the New Testament and a packet of candies. We're having a big party in the dining room, which has been beautifully decorated. There's a long table with refreshments along the wall for the happy guests. I see sausage and smoked fish sandwiches, we haven't had those in a long time, and there are butter rolls that melt in our mouths. We've completely forgotten what they taste like. And there are chocolate cookies, oatmeal cookies, candies in colorful, rustling wrappers, and fruit juices. It all tastes and looks delicious. What a respectable spread, despite the shortages of the war.

"This is my papa," Suzy introduces Papa to her friends. She's glowing with happiness, as if she's the one celebrating, and all my friends congratulate me on winning the long dress as a symbol of my excellence in Christian studies.

Each family gathers with their own communion girl. The nuns in their sensitivity celebrate with the girls who don't have any family attending.

Papa, his mouth still full of delicacies, doesn't wait to swallow before he says, "My Rita, I'm so very proud of you, and you bring me so much happiness. And Suzy, I love you so much, you've grown from being almost a baby into a happy and smart girl. You two take such good care of each other." Despite the smile of happiness on his face, his eyes are moist and his hands are clasping ours tightly, as if someone may try to separate us.

Papa suggests we go out into the yard to talk freely. The moon peeks out now and then from behind the restless clouds, bringing back memories of days gone by, and I say to Papa, "Do you remember before we left Germany? You'd come to say goodnight to me every night. And once we saw the full moon through the window and I said that it felt like it was looking at me and inviting me to come to it. Then you promised me that one day I'd fly to the moon."

"And it may just happen." Papa sighs and adds, "You're allowed to dream, you mustn't lose hope."

Suzy clings to Papa, and he pulls me into a loving hug. We stay like that for a few minutes without uttering a word until Suzy brings us back to Earth by saying, "Papa, I want to tell my friends about you but I don't know why you haven't come to visit for so long and what you do."

I give Papa a worried look while he thinks for a few moments and then answers, "You're already eight years old now, you're a big girl, and I can only tell you and Rita things that you shouldn't tell your friends. My Belgian friends and I are helping refugees, and if the Germans find out they'll arrest us. I don't visit because it puts you and me at risk. There's no need to tell your friends this. If they ask, tell them that I help the poor."

I think to myself that this is the first time that Suzy also has secrets she mustn't share, and I ask Papa, "How long will this war last? It's been going on for almost four years. We learned that eventually wars end."

"I hope that it'll end soon. The Russians are beginning to defeat the Germans, who are fleeing Russia. To the west, the Americans and the British are attacking and winning, and soon we, too, will be liberated."

"Rita and I will pray to God, Jesus, and Mary for it to happen quickly," Suzy says.

My Holy Communion and our reunion with Papa bring joy to my heart. Finally, finally I am a real Christian! The secret Suzy and I now share relieves me of the uncomfortable feeling that I'm hiding things from her. She still doesn't know that she was born Jewish but Papa did say we'd find the right time to tell her. She and I are Christians.

The guests begin to disperse and Papa says goodbye to us with a big hug and kisses while my eyes tear up and deep inside, I'm worried about when we'll get to see each other again.

Chapter 9

Another winter is almost over but it's still very cold. Clinging together, Suzy and I shiver when we stand in line for a quick wash in the morning.

"Rita, I don't remember the winter ever being so cold. Not since we've been here."

"Yes, it's very cold and I could barely fall asleep," I reply. "But I think that this winter's no colder than the ones before. The nuns are saving on heating because we're starting to feel the shortage that the war's causing. Even though it's far away from here, it still has a bad impact on us." She stares away from me.

Then I whisper, "Haven't you noticed that our food portions are smaller now, and they taste a bit bland, as if they're being stingy with the salt and there's almost no meat? The Germans are confiscating agricultural produce from the farmers and sending it to their soldiers, who are bogged down in the snow on the cold Russian front. They don't have enough coal for the trains, and on top of that the Belgian partisans are attacking them on their way east."

"How do you know?"

"I listen to the peasant women chatting in the kitchen."

I don't tell her about the whispered rumors that the Germans are confiscating the property of Jewish Belgian citizens and sending them to concentration camps to do hard labor in awful, overcrowded trains unfit to transport human beings. I listen to the women arguing among themselves whether the heretic

Jews who love only money deserve it. The women have only disdain for the Jews. They also talk about the Gestapo looking for Jews who recently escaped from the trains when they were on their way to the concentration camps. They say that the Belgian underground sabotaged and stopped them. Apparently, the Jews are hiding in the villages around us, just the way Suzy and Papa and I escaped. I'm afraid they'll come to search the convent, and I find it hard to hide my nervousness.

"I woke up this morning with a headache and feeling weak," Suzy states.

I've also been suffering from headaches for the past few days but I haven't told anyone because I thought it must be because I'm so anxious and afraid that the Germans are going to come looking for the Jews. Suzy goes to the clinic and comes right back. She's frightened by the long line of girls waiting at the clinic, they're all there because they feel weak and have headaches. There's panic and fear that it could be an epidemic, but it turns out that we're all suffering from a lack of salt in our diet. This stems from the salt shortage that the war's caused. Who would have believed it possible? Every morning after the meal we stand in line to lick salt from a nun's outstretched hand, and it takes a long time for us to get stronger because the dose is low because to the shortage. The girls are angry and whisper that it's not fair that the nuns are getting plenty of salt, and the atmosphere turns sour.

I try to understand the nuns' inappropriate behavior, and then one night the Mother Superior appears in my dream and says, "If the nuns don't get well soon, there'll be no one to run the convent, there'll be no one to take care of you and teach you."

I tell Suzy about my dream, and she tells her friends. Soon everyone knows and things calm down.

* * * *

Spring is coming, nature doesn't give war a second thought and consistently sticks to its order of operations while we stick to our routine of work, prayers, and studies.

One morning, the Mother Superior enters the classroom and says she needs help in the library arranging books that have been donated to the convent. It seems strange to me that books are being donated in the middle of a war. The Mother Superior looks at the girls who've raised their hands. They all want her to choose them, and she chooses me out of everyone. She walks fast toward the library and I follow her. At the entrance I see the edge of our priest's robe slipping away toward the exit, as if he doesn't want me to see him. There are no books in the library that need arranging. Her face worried, the Mother Superior locks the library door, and a feeling of uneasiness washes over me. My heart is predicting something ominous.

Taking both my hands in hers, the Mother Superior sits me down and says, "The priest has just informed me that two high-ranking Gestapo commanders arrived in the village yesterday evening, and there's a rumor going around that they're planning to visit the convent. We don't know exactly why, but for your safety, it's best that you stay here in the hiding place we prepared a while back to be used in case of any trouble. It's only until the reason for their visit becomes clear."

I feel the blood draining from my face and my hands start to shake. My insides are gripped by terror.

"This is only so we can protect you," she tries to reassure me. She moves a small cabinet with magazines on its shelves and I barely notice the door behind it. It's the same color as the wall. The door opens with a slight creak into a small room with a chair, a table holding a prayer book, a pitcher of water, a glass next to it, and a plate with two sandwiches. There's a picture on the wall of the Madonna holding baby Jesus in her arms.

"I'm locking the library. Don't leave the room and keep quiet.

I'll come to let you out when we know why the Gestapo officers are visiting us."

"What about Suzy?" I whisper, my lips quivering.

"You don't need to worry about her, she looks like a thoroughbred Aryan."

Her words sting but also reassure me. I hear the lock clicking, closing me in, and I shudder. I overcome the cries hankering to burst out of my mouth and I kneel before the image of the Madonna. I pray that she'll save me and I ask her to help me understand why the Germans are so evil, even though they're Christians. I promise to do better if I get out of here safely.

The sound of the lock turning makes me jump. The Mother Superior has a broad smile on her face. She's come to free me. She's like an angel sent from heaven. I run to her, throw my arms around her, and burst into tears of relief.

She strokes my head and says, "The Gestapo wants to commandeer half of the convent's unoccupied rooms and set up their regional headquarters here. They'll try not to interfere with the convent's day-to-day life."

Every time I hear the screeching of their cars when they come and go, my heart skips a beat.

Chapter 10

I always keep in mind that Jesus and Mary were also born Jewish, and even though I am now a true Christian, I'm still wary of the Germans who live in part of the convent. Deep, deep down I'm still afraid that they'll find out about my true roots and I do all I can not to cross paths with them. I don't allow Suzy to take the candy they give the girls every now and then. Even my good friend Katie stays away from them and doesn't take candy.

Our German neighbors from the Gestapo headquarters are on good terms with the Mother Superior, and they allow their military dentist to treat the girls' teeth as well. I'm terrified that the dentist, who'll get to see me from up close, will realize that I was born Jewish and I refuse to see him, even though, like many of my friends, I'm suffering from a toothache. The nun in charge makes me go. Terrified, I tremor as I sit down in the dentist's chair. From the look in his eyes, I think that he can see right through me, that he knows my secret, but he just strokes my cheek and says in German, "It won't hurt, I'll give you something for the pain."

I don't say a word, I don't reveal that I understand German. Could that be how he plans on catching me out?

My cheek swells and it hurts, but I'm here.

After seeing Papa, I have even more interest now in what's happening in the war. Until now it was far away even though we felt the difficulties in our everyday lives through reduced food rations, and of course because Mama and Papa aren't with us.

I'm very excited for my first confession this coming Sunday, and so I can't follow the priest's sermon at Mass. At the end of the service, everyone leaves, the main lights are switched off, and it's time for my confession.

A dim light leads me toward a hatch in the confessional, where our priest is waiting. I can't see him. I kneel, cross myself, and whisper in a choked voice, "Forgive me Father for I have sinned. I have bad thoughts that my mother is dead because her health hasn't improved for a long time. I haven't seen her for three years and she didn't come with Papa to the Holy Communion ceremony. I think that Papa's hiding the truth about her condition from me. I pray that she'll recover but I can't stop thinking that she's already gone."

I hear the priest shift in his chair, and after a few seconds he answers in a voice I know from our religious studies classes, "My daughter, continue to pray for her well-being and believe in eternal life in heaven for people who are good. God will grant you forgiveness and peace. I absolve you of your sin and forgive you in the name of the Father, the Son and the Holy Spirit."

I leave the confessional, kneel before the image of the Mother Mary, and pray that I won't have any more bad thoughts about Mama and Papa.

* * * *

Normal life continues but today the Mother Superior informs us that our priest is going to be replaced by a new priest. I want to ask why but she rushes out of the classroom. I'm worried because I think the priest is Papa's friend and I remember what he answered me at my first confession, when I shared my thoughts about Mama. Why did he talk about heaven? Was he hinting that something may happen to her? Is she in danger? I'm careful not to say the word "dead."

* * * *

After a few weeks of calm, in the darkness dead of night, our light suddenly comes on. It's blinding and confusing, and the Mother Superior is standing in the doorway surrounded by German soldiers in uniform, their weapons drawn. They move from bed to bed and throw off our blankets to check who's under them. We get a terrible fright, the girls around me start crying, and I understand that my fate is sealed. The damned Germans are looking for Jews. I close my eyes, cover my head with my hands so they can't see my dark hair and wait for them to find me. I hear their footsteps near my bed, they throw off my blanket, search under my bed, and move on. For a few minutes I remain frozen and the memories of that horrific day when the Germans expelled us from Antwerp and shoved us onto the train come flooding back to me. I'm terrified. Out of fear, I wet myself and my bed.

When I open my eyes, I see the Mother Superior leaving to accompany the soldiers to the other dormitories. My humiliation is revealed and a group of girls stand around me, laughing and stopping me from covering myself with a blanket. The commotion brings the Mother Superior back to the dormitory, and she understands from the girls what the matter is. She berates them, "Good Christians mustn't embarrass their friends, especially in these difficult times. I don't want to hear a single word from you about it." She adds that she'll think about the appropriate punishment for such behavior.

The Mother Superior makes the girls who mocked me confess before the priest, and to carry out the punishment he gives them too, of course. In addition, they must ask for forgiveness, not from me, but from Mother Mary. Although the story is hushed up, sometimes I think I see the nasty looks of the girls who seem happy about my shame. I'm an excellent student, constantly do Christian deeds, I have friends, and that's what's important.

But I'm afraid that I'm going to feel humiliated for a long time to come.

After the soldiers leave, the Mother Superior explains that the Germans are looking for British pilots who parachuted into the area after they shot down their aircraft.

The next day during our midday break, my good friend Katie comes up to me, hugs me, and says, "It's really not nice that the girls laughed at you, especially the ones you always help with their studies and don't allow anyone to belittle them. I also told them that it's very unchristian. It can happen to anyone, but it's not like you, Rita, because I think you're very brave. You're always the one who asks tough questions without being embarrassed. What happened to you this time?"

"You really are a good friend, so I can tell you." But I didn't tell her the truth rather what I'd planned that whole night when I couldn't fall sleep.

"One day, when I was doing kitchen duty, after that business with the way Suzy peeled the potatoes, I heard that peasant woman who never liked me say to her friends, 'Doesn't it seem strange to you that Suzy is blonde with blue eyes while her sister Rita has black hair and a nose like the Jews. They don't look at all alike. Maybe they had a Jewish neighbor.'

"The peasant women started to laugh and one of the rudest of them added that maybe it was from the Holy Spirit. A few of the other women silenced her, but others hid their nasty smirks. I've been afraid ever since, but I'm not going to tell the girls and I'll continue to behave like before—smiling, like a good, forgiving Christian."

Katie kisses me and says, "You're so brave. I love you."

Chapter 11

The year is 1944, and the battles of war are getting closer. Aircraft rumble overhead day and night on their way to bomb Germany. We are also in danger of being bombed by the Allied forces because we're in a part of Belgium that the Germans still control. The Mother Superior decides to use the cellars as a bomb shelter and we empty them, clean them, haul in mattresses, blankets, benches, and things we'll need for an extended stay. And for good reason.

But one morning, when the alarm sounds, the Mother Superior enters our classroom and asks us to go out into the yard instead of into the shelter, as the Germans have ordered. She's white as a sheet. There are a lot of frightened girls in the yard, and in the light of day we see the British aircraft hovering and circling low a few times right above us, but they don't bomb us and they disappear from the sky. Many puddles, the product of fear, are left in the yard. Katie and I exchange glances: It happens to them too.

As it turns out, the British have identified the Gestapo headquarters in the convent. Later that night, we hear the engines of the Germans' cars as they hastily leave. I feel relieved.

As the Russians and Americans advance toward our area, we hear the relentless sounds of gunfire and bombing, and we stay day and night in the shelter.

The conditions are harsh. We're overcrowded mainly at night when we put down the mattresses. There are dozens of us now, with the farm girls who are staying with us instead of returning to their unprotected homes. We don't have enough water to wash with. We can't learn when everyone's together, and how much time can a girl spend praying? We try to find something to occupy ourselves with. Much to the dismay of the nuns, our favorite game is to have races between the lice our heads are covered in. We each take one of our own and place it on the end of a piece of straw we pull out of the mattress. The first louse to finish its journey along the straw is the winner. The nuns are at a loss and try to teach us how to behave outside the convent, such as how to leave a hotel room: Tidy it up because the chambermaids aren't our servants; where to paste a stamp on the envelope of a letter, and how to write the address. Who cares? I think sinfully, but of course I keep it to myself. I can still remember our address in Germany, and I write in on the envelope I receive.

The war zones are closing in on us, the Allies are bombarding less because a few units of Germans are still not surrendering. We're gradually preparing to leave the shelter. First, only the older girls go back to their dormitories. I'm already fifteen years old, so I'm included in the group of older girls. The hardest thing is getting rid of the plague of lice and not getting re-infected. The treatment involves applying a mixture of kerosene, vinegar, and oil on our heads, three substances that are hard to obtain because of the war. With our heads bandaged and smelling pungent from the vinegar, we carry our mattresses back to the dormitories. The mattresses also need to be disinfected and we work for hours and hours in the laundry, which is all steamy from boiling our bedding and clothes. But there's hope, we can see the light at the end of the tunnel. We all pray for the final defeat of the Germans and I hope, not without worry, to see Mama and Papa soon.

* * * *

During the lunch break, my good friend Katie tells me, "The next village up from ours has been liberated, and the Germans who were still there have been taken prisoner. The Russians and Americans will be here in a couple of days. Rita, do you remember you told me that after the war you'd reveal your secret to me? You can tell me now."

"Not until the first Russian or British or American soldier enters our village and not a single German remains."

From then on, every night, before I fall asleep, I think about how to tell her. It's not an easy decision to make and I'm a little uneasy. I imagine what her reaction will be. She may hug me lovingly and say how heroic I've been, hiding my secret for so long, and now she understands why I was so afraid when the Germans were looking for the pilots. Or she may say, Rita, I'm your friend for life and you're a true Christian just as you are.

Or maybe she won't want to be my friend anymore because the Jews are bad and everyone hates them.

* * * *

After Sunday Mass, Katie and I go for a walk outside the convent. The early days of September are cool, and we're wrapped warmly against the cold. Holding hands, I whisper in her ear, "I was born Jewish."

Katie grabs her hand away. I see something unpleasant in her face. It takes a moment before she reacts angrily, "That's impossible! After all, you killed Jesus!"

I feel like she's stabbed me with a knife. She's my best friend, we've shared our most private secrets, even those about the womanhood developing in our bodies that we're forbidden to talk about, and now she's accusing me of killing Jesus? Does she think I'm less of a good Christian because I was born Jewish? That I'm worth less? That I'm a second-class Christian?

As if from a volcano that's been building up suppressed pain and frustration for years, the feeling of offense erupts from me. I move closer to her, my red face almost touching her face. She recoils in fright and I say with uncontrollable rage and in a hoarse voice that I don't recognize, "I'm a faithful Christian and a thousand times better than you. You were born into the church. You didn't choose it. You take it for granted! I made a choice, and I'm the direct daughter of God and Jesus. It's you who's worth less, to me."

Panting, I turn my back on her and slowly walk away with my head held high and my legs shaking, stifling the cry that wants to burst out of me. I go straight to the church. Kneeling before the statue of Mother Mary, I ask for forgiveness without knowing what for.

Chapter 12

The sounds of war have died down. I love the calming silence of the convent, which absorbs life through the whispers of the girls on their way to school, work, or church. I love listening to the church bells on Sundays inviting the congregation to connect with their faith. In my prayers, I thank God, his son Jesus, and Holy Mary, who saved me, but I'm slowly released from the fear that's been a constant shadow on my life for so many years. It still weighs me down and torments me in my dreams.

I have a recurring dream in which German soldiers are handing out candy and I walk away from them because I'm afraid of them noticing that I'm Jewish. One of the soldiers follows me and hands me candy. I refuse to take it and run away, but he follows me.

He catches me, and looking at me angrily, shining the flashlight on his forehead at me, he says, "Oh! I know why you're running away, you're afraid because you're Jewish!"

And I answer with a shout, "No, that's not true! It's not true!" I wake up in panic when the girl in the bed next to mine shakes me. She's angry because I'm disturbing her sleep with my screams.

Suzy and I are sure that Papa will be back soon. Every day that passes with no sign of him doesn't undermine my hope, and I get angry at Suzy, who annoys me when she says, "Ugh, why is it taking Mama and Papa so long to come back?"

I explain to her that the roads are damaged and maybe he has to first go to get Mama. I hide from her that I'm not at all sure that Mama's coming back.

The days pass but Papa doesn't come. I start to lose hope and become more concerned, until one day, I hear the peasant women talking. They heard rumors that our priest, the one who left about two years ago, was captured by the Germans along with other people, partisans, and they were seen at the station by the train going east. I remember the Mother Superior's sad face when she told us that he was being replaced by another priest. I realized a long time ago that Papa and the priest were friends and fought together as partisans against the Germans. And I now know what happened to the people who were sent to the labor camps and concentration camps, but I urge myself not to lose all hope because some of the Jews did survive.

After the war, life starts to slowly return to normal and our lives in the convent also changes. There's a lack of food and staples, and the farmers who'd been plagued by German looting and affected by the generally bad situation, take their older daughters out of school to help them rebuild their family's farm. The younger boarding school girls who have families move back home but continue their studies at the convent, which now opens its doors to homeless war orphans.

The Mother Superior calls me in for a talk, motions me to sit across from her at her desk, and says, "Rita, you're almost fifteen years old, you've completed the years of schooling that we offer. You're an excellent student, a wonderful friend, and a diligent worker. You have no family and you've waited a long time for your father to come back. You don't have a home to return to, but you can go out to work, and if you want, I'll find you a decent workplace with accommodation and pay. And we can offer you another option: You can stay at the convent for the time being and help the new girls settle in, and counsel them, like an older sister. You don't have to decide right away. Think about it. Whatever you decide, you're still under my wing."

I answer immediately, even though my eyes are filling with tears because from what she said, I understand that there's almost no chance of Papa returning.

"If Papa doesn't come back, I want one day to become a nun. Until then, I prefer to stay here at the convent and help with the new girls, counsel them, and be responsible for them. But what about Suzy? Can she stay at the boarding school?" The sobs finally escape.

The Mother Superior takes my hands and answers, "Do you remember the family that you and Suzy spent time with in the early days? They had to move you to the convent because the Germans were looking for anyone who escaped from the train. Well, they want to take Suzy in, and it's important for her to be with a family that loves her. She'll continue her studies here at our school, and you will be able to see her. I hope you'll agree to this."

I return from the Mother Superior feeling dejected and very sad. The convent is my home. I have no other.

* * * *

I put my heart and soul into guiding the impoverished girls and the war orphans. I teach them the rules of the convent and I help them with their studies and with work in the clinic. Despite the satisfaction I get from the responsible positions I've been assigned, I'm lonely. Apart from Suzy, I don't have a living soul to talk about my day with, and after work I return to my tiny room, to just me and my four walls and my picture of the Madonna. I've already reread all the stories about miracles that the convent library has to offer.

In the evenings, before I go to sleep, I'm flooded with fond old memories of home, of seeing Mama and Papa embracing each other, and I run to them and push in between them and say, "Rita, too, Rita too." And they pull me in for a big hug. I yearn for a warm touch, which I try to put out of my mind but I fail. I don't have any new friends yet. As a good Christian, I'm willing to forgive Katie and understand the reason behind what she said, but she's returned to her family and we're not in contact.

But I also have nice days, like the holidays and the days leading up to them, which are spent in preparation for them. I love Sundays in church, when I give myself over to the organ music and the choir's singing, which is so powerful it makes me forget about my everyday problems. What a shame that I'm not suitable for the choir, but Suzy represents me so wonderfully. Weather permitting, after Mass I join Suzy's family for a meal and return at sunset. Suzy walks halfway with me. She no longer complains that Mama and Papa aren't coming back, maybe because she doesn't want to make me sad, or maybe because she can feel in her gut that the chances are slim.

I'm toying with the almost improbable idea of asking the Mother Superior to join her when she travels once a month to the nearby town to run errands. I'm hoping she'll allow me to borrow books from the public library. The Mother Superior can decide what I should and shouldn't read. Day after day, I put off asking because I know that it would be overstepping and impudent to ask. This is despite knowing that she gives me special treatment, perhaps because of the friendship between Papa and the priest who both fought with the partisans. The Mother Superior did, after all, also take part in the fight against the German occupation, and in her great wisdom, she knew how to hide it. She took a huge risk hiding Jewish children.

I pluck up the courage and ask the Mother Superior for permission to borrow books, and she agrees. I eagerly devour books in German for children and youth. I prefer German to Flemish because German was the first language I ever read, and I miss it. I remember how much I enjoyed it. The selection of children's books in Flemish is limited, and I find German translations of *Tom Sawyer, Heart, Anne of Green Gables, Anderson's Fairy Tales,* and many more.

* * * *

Suzy begins the year of religious studies in preparation for Holy Communion. The shadow of Judaism is still hanging over me because I'm worried about how Suzy's going to interpret having to be baptized before her communion ceremony. Lying in bed, night after night I imagine how I'm going to tell her that she was born Jewish. I hope she'll answer me the way the Mother Superior answered me when she said that Jesus was also Jewish, but I know that's not how it's going to be. Perhaps she'll stomp her feet and scream that it's impossible, she may hit me and ask me to take it back. I feel like I've been deceiving her all these years, and that it's going to be difficult for her to understand that it's how she was protected from being captured by the Germans.

* * * *

The days pass. It's been several months since the war ended. The Mother Superior invites me to her room. She tells me that a gentleman from France who claims to be my uncle went to see the local police.

"Do you know that you have an uncle, your mother's brother who lives in France? If so, I'll show you a photograph that he left with the police so that you can confirm that he's your uncle. We want to know if you recognize him before we allow him to see you."

"Yes." I nod. "I know that my mother's brother was in France. I saw him when he visited Antwerp before the German occupation. He came to see my mother and arrange French citizenship for her, so that he could place her in a Jewish sanatorium and pay for her. Papa begged him to take Suzy and me with him to France because the Germans were on their way to Belgium. Papa said that he'd follow later. My uncle refused because his wife was against it. He said he'd already helped us by paying a lot of money for Mama's forged papers and for the sanatorium she had to stay in because of her ill health. I remember the argument they had. Papa told him not to brag about helping his sister because it's his duty and he never forgave him for giving in to his wife. And that's why, I don't want to see him," I say firmly.

Mother Superior shakes her head and answers me, "Your uncle didn't forget about you. He looked for you, found you, and came all the way here. Don't be so hasty in your decision. At least agree to see him. He's waiting in town for permission from me. I expect you to behave wisely. He's your family. Don't underestimate the family ties you've suddenly gained."

A request from the Mother Superior is basically an order.

Suzy and I walk into the library. That's where we're meeting our uncle. He's already sitting there and he stands up to greet us with a bow, and then he sits back down. Yes, it's him. His hair has gone white and he has a thin mustache, his clothes are understatedly elegant, he's wearing a gold wedding ring on one hand and a heavy gold ring on the other. His wristwatch is also entirely made from gold. He has thin-rimmed glasses, also gold, sitting on the bridge of the small hump on his nose. His hat is resting in his lap and his head is uncovered. Although he resembles Mama, he feels like a stranger to me.

The Mother Superior enters and he stands up, gives a low bow, and thanks her in German for agreeing to let him see us. She motions for him to sit down.

For a moment, an oppressive silence fills the room until Suzy asks him in Flemish, "Do you know how Mama is?"

The Mother Superior translates her question into German and the conversation is conducted in both languages.

"I thought you received the terrible news. My sister died before the end of the war and was buried in the Jewish cemetery in Antwerp. I don't know the cause of her death, but on my way back to France, I'm planning to visit her grave and say Kaddish."

I don't know what Kaddish is and I don't ask.

Suzy is dumbstruck. The skin around her upper lip goes white and I withdraw into my shell, trying to disappear and escape. Suddenly, she stares at me, points a finger right at me, and says in a choked voice, "You knew, and you hid it from me, I'm not stupid. I could feel it, that's why I stopped asking you about Mama, but did I understand correctly, she's in a Jewish cemetery? What, was I born a Jew?" Her voice changes to a scream. "Rita, answer me! Did you hide that, too, from me?"

The Mother Superior steps closer and says, "Suzy, I'm the one who wouldn't allow Rita to tell you that you were born Jewish, because that's how we saved your life. You were too young to keep it a secret if you'd known."

Suzy's breath quickens. Her forehead is covered in beads of sweat. She clasps her hand over her mouth, trying to stop the convulsions rushing through her body in waves and making her want to vomit. She jumps up and runs toward the door and I follow her. She vomits her soul and pain into the toilet. Crying, she declares, "I'm not Jewish, I don't want to be Jewish, I believe in Jesus and the Holy Mother, they're the ones who saved me."

I sit her down, wipe her face, give her a drink of water, return to the library, and deliver Suzy's message to our uncle. Speaking for myself, too, I say, "We're Christians and we believe in the Father, the Son and the Holy Spirit."

"Go back and take care of Suzy," the Mother Superior instructs me.

On my way back to Suzy, I hear the Mother Superior addressing our uncle. I stop and listen through the door.

"When you came to find your nieces, was your intention to take them in, or perhaps to adopt them?"

Our uncle replies, "I came because the Jewish Committee asked me to check if the girls are my nieces, in order to transfer them to the Jewish Committee's institutions. They locate Jewish children in convents, monasteries, and with families who hid and looked after them during the war."

The Mother Superior asks him, "Have you visited any of these institutions? Are you aware of the difficult condition the children are in? Many of them are sick or injured, and the financial situation of these institutions doesn't enable them to provide the necessary level of treatment. Rita and Suzy's father entrusted them to me, and even approved and attended the ceremonies bringing Rita into the bosom of Christianity. And soon Suzy will soon have hers. As long as they are minors, I'm responsible for them until their father returns or until they reach adulthood."

Our uncle stands up, bows again to the Mother Superior, and says in a hoarse voice, "I'm leaving my name and the names of my nieces at the offices of the Jewish Committee, and I won't bother you anymore."

That night, Suzy stays in the clinic and doesn't return to her family in the village until she recovers. I watch over her all night.

A thread of sadness lingers with her for days. She barely says a word or eats but she continues studying and preparing for Holy Communion. Tenderly, I explain to her that she first has to be baptized before the communion, and that I was also baptized, in secret because the war was in full swing and at the time there was no point in making our Jewish origin known. I don't tell her that Papa attended my baptism, only that he gave his consent, which the priest passed on to the Mother Superior.

Finally, she smiles when I remind her how happy we were when Papa came to my ceremony.

I know in my heart that there's almost no chance that Papa will attend her ceremonies as well.

* * * *

Suzy's baptism ceremony is held one morning with only the priest, the Mother Superior and myself present. I'm very sad to see Suzy's tears flowing, mixing with the water that the priest is dripping on her head. The tears and water wet the white dress covering her body, so thin and tormented it's as if she wants to make it disappear.

* * * *

The day has come, and Suzy and the other girls her age are having their communion ceremony. I recall the day I had mine, when Papa attended.

"Maybe Papa will surprise us and come to your ceremony too," I say, trying to cheer her up.

Dressed in white dresses with garlands of flowers on their heads, the girls walk onto the church stage in time to the choir and organ. Their relatives watch them, happy looks on their faces, and join them afterward at the refreshment tables. Papa doesn't come, and this time we're in the group of girls who don't have family, those who the nuns sit with. Suzy doesn't eat any of the candy she once loved so much.

Chapter 13

The silence that prevails during our midday rest on Sunday after Mass is broken by the sound of our rescuers arriving at the main gate of the church. I hear a nun's footsteps and the heavy doors creaking as she opens them, and then an unintelligible exchange of words. I hear the nun's footsteps again, this time coming toward my room.

"There's a woman asking to see you. She's speaking in a language I can't work out. She has a package addressed to you and Suzy and she showed me a document confirming that she's here on behalf of the Jewish Committee. The woman refused to give me the package. I understood that she wants to give it directly to you. I left her at the entrance to wait for you."

I meet a small woman sloppily dressed in gray. Her hair is covered with a headscarf, her mouth is pinched and the skin around her lips is very wrinkled. When she addresses me in the language that Mama never allowed Papa to speak at home—Yiddish—she exposes yellow teeth, some of which are missing. Everything about her screams misery.

She grabs both my hands and says, "*Oy meyn kind, deyn unkel hat geshikt far ir a pakat metuna fun Pariz.*" (Oh, my child, your uncle sent you a gift package from Paris.)"

She hands it to me, I take it, place it next to me, and wait.

She introduces herself and I understand only part of what she says "*Ikh arbet far di kamitet far tsurikkumen Yiddishe kinder fun manaster und fon Kristlekh mishpuches.*" (I work for the committee for returning Jewish children from monasteries and Christian families.)

"*Ikh bin du tzu fregen vost ir macht, vost ir filst und orwis nemen dig fon de finster platz vos di hust tzuzein vor di milhume. Itst mir veln dikh gefinen a goede Yiddeshe hosen und macht eine sheine hasune.*" (I'm here to ask about what you're doing, how you feel, and to get you out of this dark place that you're in because of the war. Now we'll find you a good Jewish husband and we'll give you a beautiful wedding.)

I have trouble understanding what she's saying and I ask in German, "What is *hosen* and what is *hasune*."

And she answers, "*A junger man velen dich heirten und bringen Yiddishe kinder.*" (A young man who will marry you, and you'll have Jewish children.)

I'm surprised by the suggestion, and I don't know whether to be angry or to laugh. That's all I need, to marry a Jew, I think to myself.

She continues talking and I get annoyed because I only understand some of what she's saying, and she keeps repeating certain words over and over: "*A Yiddishe kind, a Yiddishe kind.*" (A Jewish child, a Jewish child.)

She doesn't realize that I'm Christian now. She's a fool if she thinks that all it takes are a few words and a gift to convince me to join the evil Jews, who since a very long time have been persecuted for their transgressions. I lose my patience, stand up, tell her that I'm staying in the convent, thank her for the gift, and motion to the nun who's with us to escort her out. I leave the meeting and hear her clapping her hands and moaning, "*Oy gevalt, ribono shel oylam, a Yiddishe kind, rahmoines.*" (Oh no, dear Lord, a Jewish child, have compassion.) I hear deep sadness in her tone, as if she's lost something precious to her. I actually feel a little sorry for her.

I rush out to catch Suzy before she goes home to her family in the village and I ask her to stay for the afternoon and go home in the evening because I have to tell her something.

Sitting facing each other in my small cell, I find myself debating with myself over how to tell Suzy about the woman I met. She's not my old Suzy. She's changed from being bouncy and happy and has become quiet and withdrawn. She's very thin now, and her eyes are slightly sunken and red, as if she's not sleeping well.

I show her the package and say, "Our uncle from Paris sent us a gift. Do you want to open it?"

"Not on your life!" she replies angrily. "It would be better if he didn't visit or send us gifts."

"But I'm curious," I answer. I open the package containing a box of chocolates, which reminds me of past birthdays with small chocolates wrapped in gold or silver foil, just like the chocolates in this box. I hand her the open box but she refuses. I can't resist and one after the other, I devour a few chocolates.

"It's delicious, you should taste it," I coax her as I smooth out the "money wrappers," as we used to call them. My friends and I would collect them and press them between the pages of our textbooks to safeguard them. We'd compete over who had a bigger collection. Suzy was too young so we didn't allow her to smooth them out, especially not the gold ones, because she would tear or crumple them.

After her extreme reaction to the gift and her refusal to taste the chocolate, I don't have the courage to tell her about the woman who brought the package. Lately she's also been reacting with fear to stories about Jewish children who grew up with families in neighboring villages or convents. The children were taken by relatives who returned after the war or by Jewish organizations that received permission to bring them back into their old community and they sent them to Palestine. The last story we heard was about a ten-year-old girl, who as a baby was given to a family in a nearby town. She had no idea and grew up as part of the family in every way. She attended a strict Catholic school. One day after the war, relatives appeared with certified documents and demanded the girl back. The adoptive family, which had become very attached to the girl, wanted to make the separation easier for her and explained to her that she was being transferred to a boarding school to continue her studies. To her surprise, she was sent to her family in Palestine.

"I'm afraid it's going to happen to me too," Suzy tells me during our midday break.

"They know where I go to school and they'll find out which family I'm living with. I've asked to move and live somewhere else. I want to move to my adoptive family's daughter. She lives in a nearby city. She's just given birth and I'll be able to help her."

"And what about your studies? You're such a good student, I think it would be a mistake to leave school right now in the middle of the year. Aren't you overreacting a bit, being so afraid? Your adoptive family, and even more so the convent, won't allow you to be handed over."

"I'm already going on fourteen and in any case it's the last year of schooling the convent can give me. A few months doesn't make any difference. It'll be harder to find me in the city."

I try to describe to her how difficult it would be for her without friends, far from me, at home all day with a crying baby. But her mind is made up. The fear has a firm hold on her.

"I'll pray to the Holy Mother that it'll be a change for the better."

After a few minutes of silence, she says thoughtfully, "You know, Rita, I think you also need a change after spending so many years in one place."

Suzy's words echo in my mind all day long and don't relent. They hit a nerve. I've been finding it hard to admit to myself that

I'm becoming tired of my routine. The nuns, the boarding school girls, and the peasant girls who aren't really the right friends for me. I'm quite lonely and Suzy is also growing away from me—where she lives, her devout faith, and also her extreme fear. She's always praying and talking about her love for Jesus and she barely eats. It seems like she's trying to escape her physical body in order to be more spiritual. Even her fears of being taken by the Jews undermine my confidence. I'm worried.

I turn to the Mother Superior for help.

"How can I help you?" the Mother Superior gives me a warm welcome. I'm always in awe of her. My breath quickens every time I stand before her.

Last night I carefully planned what I would say but now that the time has come it all comes out in the wrong order and I find myself blurting out my concerns. "Suzy's terrified that representatives of the Jewish organizations will find her. And her fear is controlling her. She's losing her appetite and she hides from any stranger she sees. She wants to move in with relatives in the neighboring city and to help them with their newborn son. She wants your support."

The Mother Superior takes her time answering.

"I'm aware that Suzy's not doing well. It shows on her. She's losing weight and she's clearly suffering from a mental crisis. She still hasn't come to terms with the news that she was born Jewish, even though we reassured her that she's Christian in every way, both in her spiritual faith and in the baptism and Holy Communion ceremonies she had. I hope that with time she'll get over it. I'll invite her for a talk and express my support for the move." And after a short pause she adds, "And how are you, Rita? It seems to me that you're not as satisfied with your work as you were in the past."

I'm amazed at the Mother Superior's ability to pick up on my and Suzy's spirit processes. After all, there are dozens of girls at the convent. I've always felt that we receive preferential treatment, and lately I've been wondering if maybe she also has Jewish blood flowing in her veins. The thought shocks me and I quickly answer her question with some trepidation, "Suzy thinks that I, too, should leave the convent so that I won't be harassed by the Jewish organizations. And basically, I also feel that after almost a decade here, before I decide finally whether to become a nun, I should go out and get to know the outside world. At the end of the day, I feel very lonely in my tiny room, and I lack the companionship of girls my age. Yes, I do feel a restlessness of sorts."

Surprised by my own candidness, I anxiously await the Mother Superior's reaction.

As usual, she pauses a little before answering. "Surely you remember that at the time I offered to find you a job and you chose to stay in the convent. It's still an option, I'll help you. The gates of the convent will always be open to you, and I'll always be here for you."

* * * *

The Mother Superior finds me a job at an X-ray institute in Holland near the border with Belgium.

I pack my things and knock on her door to say goodbye and thank her for her help.

She motions for me to follow her to the church. She reaches into a hole on the side of the altar and pulls out a rusty iron box covered in clumps of earth. She hands it to me and says excitedly, "Your father entrusted your documents and family photos to me, to keep for you and Suzy. When the Germans settled in the other part of the convent building, just to be safe I moved them in this box to this hiding place. I think that it's time now to hand them over to you. You'll soon be eighteen. You're setting out on your own, becoming independent. Explore another option for life and then decide on your path."

Overwhelmed by emotion, I don't hold back and I hug her. She strokes my head and says, "God is with you."

Chapter 14

I find a place to live in a blue-collar neighborhood. I can walk from there to work. I have a room with a kitchenette, bathroom, basic furniture, and my own entrance. My landlord's mother used to live there. My landlord and landlady rise early for work and I hardly ever run into them. From my bedroom window I can see a small, paved courtyard, which is for my use only. It has a heavy bench that the sun visits on bright days. Not far away, there's a modest church with a small congregation on Sundays consisting mostly of elderly women with young grandchildren. I haven't met anyone around my age. Maybe they'll attend on the holidays.

On the day I arrive, while I'm arranging my meager belongings in the closet, an image pops into my mind; of my mother taking clothes out of boxes, arranging them in the closet, her face covered in tears and trying to hide that she's crying. I was about six years old. I didn't understand why the Germans had ordered and forced us to leave the beautiful home we shared with our grandparents. We moved to a poor neighborhood where the Jews of Berlin had been concentrated. I remember it was my first year in a progressive and advanced Jewish school. (That's what Papa called it.) Mama, nervous and walking fast, would accompany me to school every morning, but I'd go home on my own, always afraid to encounter the thugs in brown uniforms who would bully and beat men with beards like my grandfather's. Once in a while they would march down the street in perfect order and sing so beautifully. I watched them from behind the window and curtain, which I'd carefully pull back just a little and see the evil in their eyes. At school we received a book of poems, and written in German on the first page was: *Anstatt zu singen, sei ruhe. Bose menschen kennen keine lieder.* (Where people sing, there'll be calm. Bad people don't know songs.) But I was still very afraid of them even though they sang so beautifully. I asked Mama how this could be and she answered me impatiently, "They don't put their money where their mouth is. Beware of nice words."

* * * *

My life is completely changing. Chores that I was unaware of in the convent weigh on my new everyday life, like shopping and keeping to a budget, or preparing a meal for myself when I get home tired from work. I'm like a baby learning to walk. Life in the convent's not a picnic, but the responsibility is different. I'm unsupervised here, and my ten-year routine is completely transformed. I'm used to working hard and I've always worked diligently, but the frameworks have changed. I became lonely in the convent but the faces I saw every day were familiar and we'd exchange kind smiles. Here the people at work are polite, but at the end of the day they rush off to their families. The younger ones aren't interested in me. Their world is different from mine. They go to bars after work, hang out with young men, and tell witty jokes that I don't always understand.

Weather permitting, after work I sit on a bench in the park and watch the passersby. Sometimes a loving couple with their arms around each other will catch my eye and I'll feel a pang in my heart. I feel a need for physical closeness and affection. All the feelings that were repressed in the convent are now rearing their heads. Mothers with children make me long for a family of my own. I remember in Berlin when I would go out with Mama to the park. One of these memories, from the tougher days, is of a spring day, of Mama with a yellow patch on her sleeve not allowing me to sit on a bench in the sun because Jews were forbidden from sitting on it. I didn't understand why, and I insisted and refused to move. Mama looked around anxiously, walked away, and I had to get up and run after her.

* * * *

Suzy moves to the city to help her relative. We're waiting to see each other on Christmas for Mass at the convent church we so love, and meanwhile we stay in contact through letters.

> Rita, my sister!   December 1948
> It was so wonderful to see you for Christmas. I'm already longing to see you again. How are you? And how are you progressing at work?
> Have you already made friends? I hope so because it's very important.
> I didn't want to upset you when we met, but I'm very unhappy. The family is working me hard cleaning, taking care of the baby during the day, and also at night when he wakes up. Yesterday I fainted and the family berated me for not eating enough, claiming that that's why I'm weak. They're right, but it's hard for me to swallow when I'm feeling tired or angry at being taken advantage of. Since I don't attend school, I haven't found friends, and I really miss that. If I could, I would leave and even return to the convent, but I'm embarrassed to ask the Mother Superior, and I'm not at all sure that

it's a possibility because what would I do at the convent?

It's evening now and the baby's crying again, so I'm going to end my letter here.

Take care of yourself.

Your sister Suzy, who loves you with all her heart.

Suzy, my beloved sister, hello!   January 1949
I'm replying quickly because I've thought of a solution to your suffering and I'm going to go straight to the point. You can move in with me. We can add another bed in the room, and I'll arrange it with the landlord. Don't tell anyone you're leaving. Find the right moment. I'll send you money for train tickets and let the Mother Superior know after you arrive. She'll understand that you're better off with me than with a family you're unhappy with. It'll be wonderful to be together again. First you can help me with daily chores and then we'll find you a job. I'll make sure you don't get angry, that you eat well, and recover.
What do you think?
Yours, Rita

Dear Rita!   January 1949
What would I do without you, my good and wise sister? Your plan is wonderful. I will gladly come. I'll wait for the money and let you know exactly when I'm coming. What is your address and at which station should I get off? Wait for me on the platform. How wonderful that we'll be together.
Yours, Suzy

* * * *

Suzy leaves on Sunday right after Mass, and I wait eagerly for her. She's pale but she has a happy look on her face. To prevent anyone from noticing that she's left, she came without any luggage and wore several layers of clothing and she tucked away her personal belongings in her pockets. And still, she looks very thin.

Suzy asks to go by the church before we go home so she can thank Jesus and the Holy Mother for answering her prayers for a successful journey. I gladly join her. We kneel and I thank the Holy Mother for Suzy's safe arrival and ask for Suzy to recover from her scrawniness and fears.

When we get home, we sit on the porch and invite the landlord and landlady to join us for a refreshing drink and light refreshments, which I prepared ahead of time. They already approved the addition of another tenant, naturally for an additional payment that I can afford. The landlady is a jolly, chubby woman who has a vegetable stall in the market. Her husband works as a driver for a trucking company. They're simple, hospitable people who are happy with their lot, and with their married children and their grandchildren. The woman tells us about funny incidents, how she catches the Jewish war refugee children who are still all over the city and who steal vegetables from her stall. I squirm uncomfortably in my chair. The hatred for the Jews that I felt in the convent comes up here, too, in every conversation. I remember Papa, who was a Jewish refugee all his life.

Suzy immediately gets involved in running our modest household and relieves me of everyday concerns. She keeps the room neat and sparkling clean. Sitting together at dinner after work creates a family atmosphere. On Sundays we go to church, still dressed in our convent uniform and we're treated with acceptance and belonging to the older congregation. Suzy hangs pictures of Jesus and the Holy Mother in every corner of the room and prays in front of them at least twice a day. I, on the other hand, join the municipal library and I'm fascinated by the new world that opens up before me. I try to maintain a good level of German, the language I first learned to read in, and I soon manage to read the books that the librarian chooses for me: books for youths that haven't been translated into Flemish. Suzy doesn't support my enthusiasm for reading them and I have no partner to share these new experiences with. This reduces our topics of conversation to mainly what's happening at work, and it's a shame, but we get along. After a few weeks Suzy's face regains its color.

"I hope to be with you until I'm an adult and can join the order of nuns," Suzy shares her plans with me. "Maybe we'll go to Africa together to save the natives and introduce them to the gospel of Jesus."

I've been focusing on finding a job that'll suit her, still without success. We're planning our upcoming visit to the convent for the Feast of the Ascension.

I love Christmas Mass so much. The music and the singing choir connect me and God and make all the suffering and pain disappear. Music is a kind of magic that adds beauty and flavor to our lives.

Again, the Mother Superior welcomes us warmly. After all the services are over, she asks one of the nuns to invite us to meet with her in her room. A shadow of worry enters my heart.

The Mother Superior invites us to sit. I study her face and detect hesitation. She seems to be weighing her words.

"A few days ago, I met with an impressive man who was looking for you both. He shares your surname. He showed me documents confirming that he's your uncle and he claimed to be your father's older brother."

Suzy pales and immediately, almost together, we answer, "We refuse to meet him."

I add, "We know what his intentions are, but we're Christian."

The Mother Superior motions to me to calm down and as she gives us a stern look and shakes her head and her finger at us, she says, "I'm not finished. He's a well-known rabbi in the newly-established State of Israel. He came from Israel to meet you. I told him that you don't live in the convent and that I need to ask if you agree to see him, even though I know what your answer will be. He's waiting for an answer at a hotel in the next city. He speaks Yiddish, Polish, Hebrew, and a little German, so he came with a young translator who's fluent in Yiddish, Flemish, and Hebrew. He seems to be a man of considerable financial means and said that he's been looking for you for many months. This time you'll have to see him because yesterday he brought a court order with him. If you don't, I'll be in trouble. I told him he can meet with you today. He's waiting in the library."

Suzy bursts into tears and says, "Maybe he's an imposter!"

The Mother Superior rests her hand on Suzy's trembling shoulder and answers, "I don't think so. After all, I knew your father, and he looks a lot like him despite his beard. Come, let's go to the library."

Suzy can't calm down. Her legs are shaking and I can see how hard it is for her not to gag.

I support her as we walk to the library.

Chapter 15

As we walk into the library, we see two people scanning the books on the packed shelves. They turn to us with a slight bow. One is a stout man in his sixties. He has a white beard, a brimmed hat on his head, and he's wearing black pants and a black coat over a clean white shirt. He has a very impressive presence.

For a moment my breath catches: Oh my, he looks so much like Papa, he's only taller. He must be the uncle. A skinny man in his late twenties is standing next to him. He has a small black yarmulke on his head and small curious eyes behind the rimless glasses sitting on his big nose.

The Mother Superior invites us all to sit around the large table in the middle of the library. The leather smell of the book covers fills the room. I love the smell, it reminds me of my grandfather's big house, where we all lived before the Nazis kicked us out. Papa liked to sit in our library at home. He'd become engrossed in what he was reading and forget the problems involved in earning a living and the quarrels he had with Mama. The Mother Superior invites our uncle to speak.

He stands up, looks alternately at me and at Suzy, and says in broken German, "I'm going to speak Yiddish as it's my mother tongue as well as your father's. Apart from Yiddish, I speak Polish and Hebrew, which I presume you don't understand. That's why I brought this young man with me. His name is Volk and he's a professional interpreter with a good command of Yiddish, Flemish, and Hebrew.

"My name is Moshe Grossberg, and I'm from a Jewish family in Poland. We were eight siblings. I'm your father David Grossberg's oldest brother. He was ten years younger than me. I was ordained as a rabbi and I was a rabbi in the Polish army. When Poland was occupied by the German Nazis, my wife, our four children, and I, had to move to the Warsaw Ghetto. Thanks to my connections with Polish friends, I was able to get out of the ghetto and worked to get my wife and four children out as well."

His voice is tremoring and I think his eyes are wet.

"I was too late. They were sent to an extermination camp. I failed. To this day I feel guilty that they're not alive and I'm standing here before you. I won't go into the details of how I escaped from Poland, and how after many difficulties and hardship I arrived in Palestine before the end of Second World War. I've been searching for years for any surviving relatives, until I found out about you." He falls silent.

I interrupt his silence and ask, "And what happened to your other siblings?"

"Only two of us survived. Apart from me, Dov the youngest of the boys lives in Israel. He was thirteen when he made it from Poland to Palestine with our parents—your grandparents—before the Second World War. Our brother Jacob, like your father, distanced himself from religion and was rebellious in nature. He volunteered to fight in the Spanish Civil War and he didn't return. All the others remained in Poland and perished."

Despite the sad story, Suzy says defiantly and with a hint of cruelty, "It hurts to hear that you lost your family. Unfortunately, you're too late now as well. We're Christian and have no interest in Israel or in being Jewish."

I'm surprised by her direct statement, as are Uncle Moshe and the Mother Superior. He watches her solemnly and answers, "I won't hide my hope that you'll return to our people, but as a person of faith I know that others cannot be forced to change their faith. Right now, it's important to me that you know that you have a family that'll welcome you with open arms and help you if necessary. You aren't alone in the world. I would love us to get to know each other better. I'll be staying here for a while longer, and I hope you'll agree to continue meeting with me, always in the presence and with permission of the Mother Superior."

The Mother Superior gets up and signals that the meeting is over and asks to see us without Uncle Moshe and after we have a short rest.

I'm afraid that the Mother Superior is going to reprimand Suzy for her harsh words, but happily she doesn't mention it. She looks at me and says, "Family is very, very important. You can be proud to have Uncle Moshe, an educated and very impressive man who reminds me of your father. If your father had returned and found you, you would certainly have returned to your people, who lost six million souls. Your father was not a religious man, but during the war, which is an abnormal reality, he saved you as Christians. I think you should live among the people and family who want you. If you want, you can live as Christians in Israel, where there's freedom of religion and convents. Think about what I'm saying. I'm going to allow your Uncle Moshe to continue meeting with you so that you can get to know each other better and you can explain to him your position on continuing and strengthening your family bond." With that, she signals that the meeting is over.

I'm left feeling confused and Suzy looks shocked. I feel slightly betrayed. The convent and the Mother Superior are home to me, the place where I grew up. I, at least, have memories of our old home with Papa, but for poor Suzy there is no other place. Is the Mother Superior trying to get rid of us? That can't be. Maybe she promised Papa that when the day comes, we'll be allowed the opportunity to decide who we are.

* * * *

This morning we have another meeting. After a few minutes of silence, the Mother Superior signals to the interpreter to begin the meeting.

"Good morning" he addresses us in Flemish. "You heard Uncle Moshe's hope that you'll return to your people and continue your relationship with him. It's important for us to understand more deeply how you feel."

Suzy sits there with pursed lips and I see in the Mother Superior's expression that she expects me to answer Volk.

I answer and say, "I've always known that I was born into a Jewish family. I have dim memories of the welcoming of the Sabbath that my grandparents held when we lived with them. Our grandmother would say a blessing over the candles and our grandfather would say the blessing over the wine."

His interest sparked, Uncle Moshe raises his head, as if expecting good news.

"But," I add, "Papa wasn't like them. He refused to do as Mama asked and attend synagogue. I remember him relenting once after arguing vehemently with Mama when she mentioned Yom Kippur several times. Mama insisted that I go with him, probably as a spy to make sure that he did as she asked. On the way back from the synagogue he told me, 'I'm a secular Jew,' and I asked, 'What's secular?' 'A heretic,' he replied. 'A person who doesn't observe commandments and doesn't believe in a God whose orders must be obeyed.' Then I asked, 'At the Jewish school in Antwerp they told us that God will protect us if we keep the Sabbath and His commandments. So, Papa, who is right, you or the teacher?' To this he replied without explaining, 'Every person should live according to his own beliefs.'"

"And what do you think today?" Uncle Moshe asks, who until now hasn't interrupted me.

"I know that the God of the Jews didn't protect us. All my childhood memories are accompanied by constant fear because of being Jewish. The fear sparked by the windows in Jewish stores being smashed, the fear of Jewish homes being burned down. The fear of Mama going shopping with the little money we still had because Papa was a refugee without citizenship and couldn't find work. The fear I felt on the way to school and on the way back, hoping that they wouldn't notice me, that the police officers in the green car that drove around the neighborhood wouldn't come to our home and take Papa away."

I sigh deeply and tears fill my eyes as I remember one particular memory. "One day, I dared to tell Mama that I didn't want to be Jewish and she answered me with a stinging slap. Crying, I told her that if they hate the Jews so much, it means that they're bad and that God doesn't love them. Mama started crying and I became frightened by what I said because my father was a good man and I loved him so much. To this day, I've only suffered from the fact that I was born Jewish. All my life in the convent, all ten years, I was afraid that the girls would find out that I was born Jewish. Even today, as a Christian who believes with complete faith in Jesus and the Holy Mother and that they are the ones watching over me, I'm still not comfortable with my origin and I hide it."

The silence in the room is heavy. No one responds.

Volk the interpreter looks at Suzy, who doesn't open her mouth.

I answer for her, "In complete contrast to me, Suzy didn't know or remember. She grew up as a Christian, without fear. Discovering her origin so suddenly shook her so badly that she truly suffered both emotionally and physically, and the fear that I had all my life penetrated her too. Her fear, however, isn't of the Germans but of the Jews kidnapping her."

Emotional and exhausted by speaking so much, I cover my face with both my hands and burst into tears.

Suzy gets up from her seat, comes to me, and hugs me. "Rita, my sister, I love you," she says. "You understand my soul."

The Mother Superior stands up. The meeting ends.

Chapter 16

Our last meeting with Uncle Moshe was terribly exhausting. We said everything that was on our minds and as such I have no interest in seeing him again. But today, too, after Sunday Mass, we get together again. Suzy and I get to the library early and wait.

Restless, Suzy mutters, "Ugh, what else does he have to say, and that Hebrew has a terrible sound to it."

She falls silent when the Mother Superior, Uncle Moshe, and the interpreter enter together. They all seem content, which worries me. The Mother Superior motions to Uncle Moshe to speak.

He stands up and says excitedly, "Dear Rita and Suzy, I was impressed by what you said and I respect your decision to keep your faith and not return to your roots. I feel great affection for you and ask that you always consider me your family and a person who'll act in your interest." He stops and turns his gaze to the Mother Superior, as if asking for her permission to continue.

The Mother Superior nods her head in agreement.

"Rita," he continues. "You just turned eighteen and I want to give you and Suzy a birthday present. A present that I would have liked to have given to my own children, but I can't. I'm offering you a trip to Paris, and to return to Antwerp from there by sea. We'll part ways in Antwerp and you'll go back home. After spending almost ten years at the convent, before you decide on your future path, this is an opportunity to get to know a world that's different from yours. I discussed this with the Mother Superior. She gives her permission regarding Suzy, who's still a minor, but I need your consent because you're already an adult."

Overwhelmed by surprise, I'm speechless and don't know how to respond. The Mother Superior comes to my aid, "You don't need to answer right now. Talk to Suzy. If you feel the need, I'll be happy to discuss it with you without Uncle Moshe present. He'll wait for your answer."

Suzy pulls me into the yard we so love; the convent yard where we spent the spring days of our childhood. We would meet after Sunday Mass to tell each other about our week. We look at the same green fields, hear the same ringing of the bells around the necks of the cows lying in the meadow, and the same silence that's broken from time to time by the church bells calling people to church. The silence becomes stronger when the bells fall silent.

I sink into thoughts about the past. We didn't always have it good. The convent rules were strict and the physical work was hard. I spent most of my days in fear, but I had the belief that someone was watching over us. Sometimes, when the nuns became angry with children who found the strict discipline and work too difficult, they would become cruel, but Suzy and I were treated particularly well. Perhaps because we weren't peasant girls, or perhaps for other reasons that I'm still trying to understand. Along with memories of feeling afraid and of hard work and strict discipline, I also have many fond memories, of doing well in my studies, of good friends, and fun holidays. Now I face other times, difficult days of having to protect the identity I developed in the convent from shattering, of protecting myself from the nagging questions regarding who I am, and from the immense mental upheaval that Suzy's facing.

Suzy interrupts my thoughts and says, "Even though our uncle's offer is very tempting, I'm going to turn it down. I'm under the impression that our uncle is trying to atone for his guilty conscience over not being able to save his family more than having our interests at heart. And perhaps he still hopes to bring us back into the Jewish fold."

It takes me a while to digest Suzy's wise words and I reply, "There's a lot of truth in what you're saying. Still, that's no reason not to join him on the trip. Think of the times you imagined joining a mission in Africa and saving the souls of the natives who would then begin to believe in Jesus. Like you, he's also acting like a missionary. Our faith is strong and we shouldn't be afraid of him. The Mother Superior has left the decision to us, but she's not hiding her opinion that we should accept the gift. Will someone ever again offer us such an expensive gift? Will we ever be able to afford such a trip?"

Suzy's face becomes sad, she sighs, and replies, "Wait until tomorrow before you give them an answer. I understand that you're inclined to accept our uncle's offer. Just so you know, if you decide to agree, I won't leave you, I'll come along on the trip, despite how deeply uneasy it makes me feel. You're the only family I have."

I decide to accept our uncle's offer.

After saying goodbye to the Mother Superior, we go back home. Uncle Moshe and the interpreter Volk pick us up after Uncle Moshe pays two months of our rent, one for the month we'll be away and another to tide me over until I get paid again, since I'll be taking vacation from work. It's all been approved. Uncle Moshe efficiently handles all the details.

We have a first-class compartment on the train to Paris all to ourselves. With her head on my shoulder, Suzy dozes uneasily while I look at the changing scenery, bask in the smell of the fields, and recall two previous train trips I took: The first, when we were frightened and unaccompanied little girls leaving Germany to meet Mama and Papa who were waiting for us in Antwerp. And the more horrific trip, when the Germans shoved us into the carriages packed with terrified people. I remember how much I regretted playing with the cardboard doll and her cutout paper clothes, which I lost when we disembarked on the tracks after they were blown up by the partisans. I loved that game so much that despite the terror of being deported at dawn, I put it in a small bag along with a book to read and kept it close to me. That is, until I dropped it when we escaped in panic and ran into the fields.

I check repeatedly if the documents, which Papa gave to the Mother Superior for safekeeping, are in my bag, that I didn't forget them when I packed for the trip.

Dressed in our convent uniforms, a prominent cross around our necks, we decided that this is what we'd wear for the entire trip. It's almost Thursday evening when we arrive at the hotel in Paris. We're tired after hours of being shifted from place to place. We had to be on time for the train from Amsterdam that stopped at the station near our apartment.

"What a beautiful room," Suzy says.

I spread out on the big, wide bed. "Wow," I exclaim. "The mattress is so soft, I'm literally sinking into it."

The memory of my mother's perfume on our sheets is so strong that I can smell it, and I remember how I used to jump into Mama and Papa's bed on Saturday mornings. Suzy and I would compete for the closest spot, pushing each other until we found our positions, mine between Papa's big muscular legs. I'd lie on my back with my head on his stomach and Suzy would lie between Mama's soft legs.

Suzy, on the other hand, takes out the picture of the Madonna and Jesus and hangs it on the wall above her bed. As soon as we walk in, she kneels to pray. I can barely force myself to join her. From the other room we hear Uncle Moshe and Volk muttering their prayers. When we're done praying, I share a thought with

Suzy, that we and our uncle pray to the same God, except that our Messiah has already arrived and that of the Jews has been delayed and they're still waiting for him. Suzy grimaces. She doesn't like such talk.

Dinner is brought to our room. Volk asks if we don't have any issues with the hotel's kosher food. I answer that we don't have prohibitions like the Jews and I remember that in the days of the Nazis we didn't have enough food because Mama insisted on kosher meat, which was banned by the Germans, and we didn't have enough money to buy it on the Jewish black market. This was another reason for Mama and Papa to argue. Papa screamed in frustration, "You're suddenly so righteous, as if God will notice you and save you from German persecution." All these arguments would end with Mama bursting into tears and then locking herself in the bathroom.

We all say a blessing before the meal, each of us according to our own faith.

Chapter 17

It's already Friday and our first morning in Paris. Not wanting to wake Suzy, I stay in bed and look around our room. It's large and has a high ceiling and wooden shutters, the slits of which are slightly open and dimming the morning light. Our big, heavy, separate beds are standing side by side. The bed linen is sparkling clean and the pillows are big and luxurious. And the mattress, it's so soft. A heavy square, solid-wood table and two matching wood chairs are in the middle of the room. On the dresser by the wall, there are leaflets and a small leather-bound book, perhaps the Old Testament or a prayer book. There's a stylish full-length oval mirror on one of the wardrobe doors. None of the furniture is new but it's all well preserved, as if it's the stepchildren of the fancy furniture in our grandfather's house in the good old days.

I'm not used to staying in bed after waking up. For all my many years at the convent, rain or shine, every morning I'd have to catch a spot at the head of the queue for a quick wash in cold water if I didn't want to be late for morning prayers and breakfast. We were punished if we were late.

I rush to the bathroom and shout enthusiastically to Suzy, "Suzy, get up, you won't believe it, we have hot water in the shower." What a treat. Not believing that such a pleasure even exists and feeling slightly sinful, I surrender myself to the flowing water.

Volk asks us through the door if he and Uncle Moshe can join us for the late breakfast that'll be brought to the room.

Uncle Moshe, all smiles and good morning wishes, sits down to eat with us and Volk. He asks if our room is comfortable and how we slept. I answer nicely that the room is cozy and comfortable and that we slept well after the tiring day. Suzy barely says a word. Uncle Moshe apologizes that he won't be able to join us today because he has a few things to take care of, he'll meet us in the evening. He's leaving us in the trustworthy hands of Volk, who is also fluent in French.

We visit a few tourist sites around the city. The spring weather has flooded the city with tourists, and like everyone else we stand in a long queue to go up the Eiffel Tower. We can see the entire beautiful city from the top of the tower, bright white squares and blooming gardens wherever we look. My eyes strain to take in the sights and store the spectacular abundance to memory. Church towers stand tall and seem to have been waiting here all these years for me to visit and pray in them. I take deep breaths and thank God for bringing me this far and allowing me to make sacrifices for Him.

Our next stop is the Louvre Museum. At Volk's recommendation, we focus on only a few masterpieces and on the Impressionists. Volk explains the paintings, giving them some background and new depth. Everything is impressive and so different from what we're used to.

There's a large crowd around the *Mona Lisa* blurting out automatic sounds of admiration. Waiting to see the famous painting from up close, Volk tells us that it was painted five hundred years ago by the famous painter, Leonardo da Vinci.

The painting is beautiful but I don't really understand why it's so highly regarded. I keep that to myself. Who am I to judge?

Suzy, who apparently feels the same as me or can guess what

I'm thinking, asks, "Volk, what's the secret of this painting? What makes it so captivating?"

Volk pauses before giving us a long explanation, "Artists have always wondered who she was, is she smiling, what she's hiding in her hands, and whether she's a lady or engaged in the most ancient of professions. In my opinion, she's simply a beautiful, attractive woman who's interesting to look at. There's something pleasing in the proportions of her face and the play of light and shadow adds a level of mysteriousness to her character. People who understand aesthetics attribute this to the Golden Ratio dimensions of her face, the division of its length by its width."

I, on the other hand, am more fascinated by Claude Monet's *Rouen Cathedral* series of paintings, with the colors and shadows surrounding it changing throughout the day. I sit down on the bench in front of the paintings to absorb their beauty until Volk suggests moving on. In his opinion, an hour in the museum is above and beyond in order to absorb the exhibits well.

We take a cab to the Champs-Élysées. The boulevard's wide sidewalk looks to me like a huge café, with the crowds of people sitting at round tables and drinking cold or hot drinks and eating sweet or savory pastries. The vast variety makes it hard for me to decide what to order. Volk, who we discover is a man of the world, orders for us. We start with a baguette sandwich with melted cheese peeking out and we finish with what Volk calls a classic vanilla eclair. I feel elated. Suzy agrees that it's delicious but she can't eat much, her stomach has shrunk. I feel sorry for her. Volk is content with drinking coffee on the grounds that we have a big dinner waiting at the hotel. We look at the boulevard that's full of speeding cars of all sizes and colors, and also at the people eating or just passing by. They're dressed in a variety of colors and the women are so beautiful and elegant. I wonder out loud if nobody in Paris works. It's lunchtime, Volk, our guide defends the Parisians, adding that many of the people are tourists like us.

We take the metro back to the hotel. It's scary and has a strange, unpleasant smell. For me and Suzy it's our first introduction to the underground beast. With sore feet and tired but marveling eyes from the multitude of experiences we've had, we fall on our soft beds.

Volk informs us that dinner will be a traditional Jewish Friday evening meal to welcome the Sabbath and we're invited to join. I vaguely remember Friday evenings when our grandmother would say the blessing over the candles and our grandfather would say the blessing over the wine.

When it's time to get ready, we put on our festive convent uniform and go down to the dining room. Uncle Moshe stops us at the entrance whispers to us to please hide our crosses so we don't offend the hotel's religious guests. I feel very uncomfortable with his request but I remember that Papa used to say, "When in Rome, do as the Romans do." Reluctantly I put the cross under the collar of my dress but Suzy doesn't respond. Uncle Moshe repeats his request.

Suzy answers him angrily, "The cross is me and I cannot hide myself."

Torn between my fear of Uncle Moshe and Suzy's anger, I freeze.

Suzy turns her back and returns to our room as she exclaims at me, "What is wrong with you? That's not how a faithful Christian behaves."

Uncle Moshe whispers in my ear, "I understand, join her, she's your sister."

I return to the room and find Suzy crying. I stroke her head and say, "My sweet Suzy, you have no reason to cry. You're the brave one here, I'm the weak one."

Hoping to help her feel better, I tell her that Uncle Moshe told me to join her in our room. "Please forgive him. His intention wasn't bad." Then my imagination steps in and I add, "I'm sure he had no choice. It's better not to take part in the Sabbath dinner than to cause a commotion in the hotel and find ourselves being asked to leave."

A few minutes later, there's a knock at the door. I open it. It's a waiter with two trays piled with delicacies. He puts them down on the table.

The aroma of soup fills the room. It smells familiar to me. It smells like my grandmother's clear chicken noodle soup.

"Get up Suzy, let's eat, it's our grandmother's soup."

But she stays on the bed. The aroma of the soup is calling to me. I can't resist it and I can't wait for her. It has a mild taste and it fills my stomach with warmth. I noisily suck the noodles in with my lips and smile when I see Mama's image. She always forbade me from eating like that, pointing out that it's impolite. The plum compote is as sweet as the distant taste of my childhood and of better times. My grandmother's chopped liver was tastier, but I eat it all up together with chunks of challah bread, which I break off with delight until the very last crumb.

I mutter to myself, "Oh, what did I do? There's only one challah. I didn't leave any for Suzy."

She's still sprawled on the bed, weak but less agitated now. I go over to her and prop her up on her pillows. I can feel how skinny she is. I bring the soup to her and feed her spoon after spoon until she calms down. She tastes the plum compote she loved so much as a child, but she can't finish it.

I ask for tomorrow's breakfast to be brought up to the room.

Because it's the Sabbath, we don't visit the city. Volk explains that Uncle Moshe went to the synagogue and is now taking his usual afternoon rest. He suggests we go to the nearest park. We sit on a bench surrounded by weeping willow branches. There are people walking their dogs, and in contrast we don't see any mothers pushing strollers.

After a few minutes of silence, I ask Volk to give me and Suzy some space so that we can talk freely. "I see you slept well last night," I begin, "I'm glad you ate breakfast. Are you ready to talk about what happened last night?"

Suzy's face contorts in pain. It seems that she's been waiting for this moment to unload the weight on her heart.

"I can't believe that you agreed to hide your cross! Moreover, you defended Uncle Moshe and told me that he told you to follow me to the room. You don't understand, that makes it even worse because it didn't come from you to be loyal to me and to your faith!"

I cover my face and say, "Suzy, you're so right and I'm really ashamed. I didn't know what to do. I hid the cross because I was afraid there would be a commotion and because of us Uncle Moshe would be embarrassed. And I really should have been the one to say gently that we both wouldn't join them for the meal. Maybe I'm not a good enough Christian and I'll ask for forgiveness when we attend Sunday Mass tomorrow, here in Paris."

Suzy grabs my hands and says excitedly, "And we'll pray to always be faithful to each other, to Jesus, to Mary, and to our Father in heaven."

"Amen."

Chapter 18

Suzy and I are excited because we'll be attending Sunday Mass at Notre Dame Cathedral. The nuns told us all about this wonderful church. It's construction began in 1200 BCE and took about two hundred years, but we never imagined that we'd ever get to see it with our own eyes and pray in it.

Volk, his knapsack on his back, is ready to leave and urges us to get to Mass early before it gets too crowded with people coming to pray or with sightseers. We come out of the metro station by the church to see two tall, impressive towers. They're rectangular in shape and there's a huge rosette stone between them. It looks like the towers are holding it between them. The towers and rosette are resting on a row of statues of people wearing crowns on their heads. Volk explains to us that they are the twenty-eight kings of Israel and Judah. Below them are the cathedral's three entrance gates, the top of which looks like pointed bonnets.

The church bells suddenly break into the space, ringing to invite people to Mass. Their power echoes and rolls into the distance and on its way pulls on the strings of my soul. I sneak a peek at Suzy. Her eyes are moist with emotion. We quickly enter the church.

Volk calls out to us, "I'll wait for you here at the entrance. I'll recognize you by your clothes. If for any reason we don't manage to meet up, take a cab to the hotel."

Volk hands us money and a card with all our hotel's details and adds kindly, "The money will also be enough for food and drink if you get hungry. Be careful of pickpockets and cute, friendly gypsy children."

Suzy and I hold hands and walk toward the cathedral prayer hall. I'm awestruck by the vast space and its dim lighting, which amplifies its dimensions. But the huge, impressive hall also makes me feel distant from my God. I'm used to a small, intimate church where I feel close to those I pray to. The transition from the cathedral's gray stone external facade to the purple, blue, red, and white stained-glass windows is surprising and mesmerizing. And above them all, the huge rose window wins with its beauty and light filtering through it to create a dreamlike atmosphere.

A large crowd fills the prayer hall. The high ceiling dwarfs the people sitting on the many benches along and across it. The stage is far from the front row seats and there are sparkling white marble steps leading to it. We find free seats at the back of the hall and hold hands in anticipation of Mass.

A powerful male choir and organ fill the entire hall and a priest in a pink robe begins the service with a sermon in French, which I don't understand. A white-robed priest walks across the stage waving the incense. I close my eyes, enjoy the choir's bewitching singing, and thank Jesus and Mother Mary for bringing me this far.

Suzy's hand gently loosens its grip on mine. I open my eyes and look at her. Her eyes are closed, her mouth is slightly open, like a baby's, and she has a sweet smile on her calm face. There is so much happiness on her face, as if she's feeling the touch of the Holy Mother's hand. Without putting it into words, I feel that this is her place, her world, the world of faith. It's my duty to protect her. Will I manage to?

That's the essence of what I pray for in this Mass.

Clicking cameras and exclamations of admiration from people passing through a wide opening in one of the distant corners of the hall interrupt my thoughts and bring me back to reality.

The service is over. The crowd flows out but we stay behind to light candles. We catch a glimpse of Volk, who's making his way toward us.

We decide to take a look at the cathedral from the outside, with its many spires, statues, gargoyles, and the embedded round stone in the concrete of the public square, which according to Volk is a geographical marker that the distance from Paris to all other places are measured. It is common belief that anyone who stands on it is guaranteed to return to Paris.

Without warning, the sky darkens and torrential rain surprises us. It turns into a light drizzle and doesn't stop. Volk takes a folded raincoat from his knapsack, hands it to me, and asks me to help Suzy into it. While I am, he opens and holds his umbrella over me, and then hands it to me. He takes another umbrella out of his knapsack for himself. Volk thought of everything. I really like the gesture. It feels like we have an older brother who's looking after his younger sisters. We wade through the water in our sandals, and our clothes are now a little wet. With no choice, we forgo a walk around the church's island and decide to return to the hotel, drenched but in good spirits.

On the way there, Volk asks us what we thought of the church. Suzy, who doesn't often share her feelings with Volk, surprises me. "The music, the music, how I love church music!" she exclaims.

"If so," Volk answers. "We'll change our clothes, have a bite to eat, and visit the church with the most heavenly music of all, the Church of St. Eustache. And from there, in the evening, we'll visit the Basilica of Sacré Coeur, the Basilica of the Sacred Heart, which is located on the top of the highest hill in Paris. There's a particularly spectacular view from there."

Drunk from the music and stunned by the view, we return to the hotel without uttering a sound. In our room, we kneel to thank our God for the wonderful day we're having.

Chapter 19

Light knocking on the door is followed by Volk's voice announcing, "Your breakfast is on a tray by the door. Today we're going shopping in the huge Galeries Lafayette. Uncle Moshe and I will be waiting for you at the hotel entrance."

This is the first time since we've been in Paris that Uncle Moshe is coming sightseeing with us. My enjoyment of breakfast is tinged with apprehension over how he and Suzy are going to interact after that incident on Saturday night. They haven't seen each other since. Suzy, as usual, eats little. She also looks worried and blurts out, "What do we need to go shopping for? I'd rather see other beautiful places."

"How are we going to walk around in our sandals? They still haven't dried properly after the downpour yesterday. Besides, I'd like to buy gifts for the Mother Superior, our landlord and landlady, my co-workers, and even a few souvenirs for ourselves."

I debate how to ask Suzy not to scowl at Uncle Moshe so that the atmosphere isn't ruined. Feeling that I have something to say, she beats me to it, "Well, really Rita, say what's on your mind already. Your face is giving you away. You're afraid of the way I'm going to be with Uncle Moshe. I don't think we should agree to everything Uncle Moshe asks of us if it goes against our faith. I'm sure that the Mother Superior didn't dare ask him to take his brimmed hat off when he entered the convent, so I think asking us to hide our crosses was unbearably arrogant and inconsiderate."

"I agree, he was insensitive to us. He made a mistake by not explaining beforehand how he expected us to appear in the dining room. If he had, we could have explained to him that his request was inappropriate. He's a wise man and now he understands what he can and can't ask of us. His goal is to bring us closer to the people he thinks we belong with. He's like the missionaries who go to Africa to introduce the natives to Christianity, except that we aren't primitive natives, and he's not going to succeed."

Suzy answers me angrily, "I feel that you're too understanding of him, definitely much more than he is of us. What, then, do you want from me?"

"I'm just asking you to soften your words. Use a smile instead of anger. Respond flexibly and moderately. Do you remember when you said you wanted to be a missionary in Africa to bring the natives closer to believing in Jesus? That was your dream. I can imagine you surrounded by a large group of half-naked natives with a missionary who knows their language to translate what you're telling them about the punishments that God will give them if they don't follow the ways of His son Jesus." Then I burst out laughing, ask Suzy not to be angry with me, and add, "I imagine the natives being afraid of what you're telling them, getting angry, and boiling you in their soup pot."

Suzy sees nothing funny in this but at least it doesn't make her angry. I breathe a sigh of relief and hope that she got the message.

The shopping center is a few minutes' walk from the hotel, so we stroll down the impressive Boulevard Haussmann. Even before we reach the entrance, we're impressed by the splendor and beauty and by the colorful shop windows. I stop in surprise at the entrance when I see how immense it is, especially the high ceiling, a dome constructed entirely from colored glass windows. A yellow light filters through them, illuminating the dozens of stands offering thousands of items...perfumes in beautifully designed bottles, makeup, brushes, purses in dozens of shapes and colors, sheer colorful scarves, dazzling jewelry. Our eyes feel exhausted from trying to absorb the abundance. Despite how early in the day it is, a long line stretches toward the repetitive clinking of cash registers entering the prices of the basketsful of goods.

The atmosphere reminds me of yesterday, when a large crowd was waiting for morning Mass at Notre Dame, but in contrast, those people wanted to be close to something more spiritual than buying objects, some of which seem completely extravagant to me.

Looking for sandals, we go up the stairs to the women's shoe department on one of the upper floors, but there are no bulky sandals like ours. The saleswomen kindly direct us to the men's shoe department. Uncle Moshe suggests that we go back to the women's department and also buy clothes and comfortable walking shoes. We go willingly.

I notice that Uncle Moshe is walking at some distance from us, perhaps to avoid the surprised looks of many people when they see us in our clothes next to our companions, in theirs.

"Let's go to the games department and choose a few to occupy us on the long cruise back to Antwerp."

I remember my cardboard doll and her paper clothes, the game I so loved and lost on the train the Germans deported us on. Many years have passed, and the memory of losing it still stings my heart.

We hardly ever played in the convent. We were even forbidden to jump rope for reasons of modesty, and were punished if we did. Sometimes we played ball games and jumped on the squares we drew in chalk on the courtyard stone tiles. As seniors, we didn't play at all.

I find myself standing in the middle of the huge store, at a loss because I don't know any games other than dolls and balls. I stop by the dolls and feel like a little girl being taken to a fairy tale land. There are so many dolls, with long, short, black, and blonde hair, with black and blue eyes, dressed and naked, big and small, and I don't know which to choose. My new sandals are hurting me, my eyes are hurting, I'm short of breath, my head starts spinning, and everything starts circling around me. I try to steady my failing legs and lean against the wall.

Suddenly I think I see someone taking down a large box with a doll from one of the shelves. Is it Papa? He looks so much like him. Yes, it's my father, that's the doll he gave Suzy so that she wouldn't disturb me when I played with my cardboard doll. I rub my eyes and repeatedly tell myself, that man is my father. I try to get closer to him but my legs can't hear me. He walks quickly to the cashier at the far end of the hall.

I call out to him, "Papa, it's me, Rita, when did you come back? Suzy's here too, it's me Rita." He's swallowed up in the crowd and disappears. I feel a tearing pain inside, like a knife stabbing me.

My body shrinks, tears flood me, and then I hear Suzy say, "Rita, what's the matter? Why are you yelling? You're scaring me, you're shaking, and you're so pale." She holds my arm so I don't fall, calls Volk who gives me water from a bottle he takes out of his knapsack, and they both lead me to the nearby cafeteria.

Volk brings each of us a large glass of orange juice and a croissant. He sits down next to us and says, "Rita, this is freshly squeezed natural juice, it'll help you to feel better quickly. Could you have caught a cold when you got wet in the rain yesterday?"

I noisily slurp all the juice up through the straw. I start to feel better, and while I'm happily biting into the croissant, I answer Volk with a smile, "You have nothing to worry about. In the convent we would plod through icy snow water to pick the asparagus and I never got sick, so a few drops of rain won't affect me. I was feeling a little faint, from the suffocating dry air."

"I hope you're right. Wait for me here in the cafeteria and I'll take care of the games."

When Volk leaves us, I say to Suzy, "I don't remember every drinking fresh orange juice."

Suzy takes just a few sips and says, "It's very tasty, but I can't finish it. You can also finish my croissant."

I don't try to persuade her otherwise and I greedily gobble up her leftovers. Suzy watches me devouring the food and asks, "So what happened to you? I'm not used to seeing you barely able to stand."

"Do you remember my cardboard doll?" I ask her. "You used to scream when I didn't let you dress her in her paper dresses. Papa brought you a real doll, not a cardboard one, and mom sewed clothes for her. They hoped it would stop the fights. But that didn't really help because what you truly wanted was the cardboard doll."

"I vaguely remember, but what does that have to do with it?"

"I don't really understand it myself. I was a little confused from the suffocating hall, and I thought I saw Papa with the doll he brought you. Then he disappeared, like in a dream that begins with hope and ends with utter disappointment."

Suzy doesn't say a word, she just strokes my hand and her eyes radiate love.

Volk returns with a loaded knapsack and says, "Rita, I'm glad the color's back in your face. Is there anything the two of you want to buy? Underwear, perhaps, or clothes?"

"No, we've brought everything we need. We'll just pick up a few gifts and souvenirs."

We leave with a bag of different models of the Eiffel Tower, a large rolled up unframed picture of Notre-Dame, keyrings with models of the Arc de Triomphe, and a small figurine of Jesus with Mother Mary. Volk's knapsack is full to capacity and Uncle Moshe is loaded down with huge carrier bags bearing the Galeries Lafayette logo.

"We're going back to the hotel," Volk informs us. "We'll eat, rest, and in the afternoon, we'll take a cruise along the Seine River. Tomorrow morning, we'll say goodbye to Paris with a comprehensive bus tour of the city, then we'll return to the hotel to pack, and take a train to the port."

Chapter 20

During breakfast, before we leave for the cruise on the Seine, Suzy looks at me for a long time, noticing how much I'm enjoying the fresh rolls and fragrant plum jelly that I've spread generously on them. I notice her hesitation before she says, "You know Rita, a good Christian should eat less. You probably remember what the nuns always told us: 'Overcome the pleasures of the body.' You've really gone too far this trip."

I know that she's right. I nod my head in agreement and bow my head. I don't have an answer. I'll confess to the priest as soon as the trip is over. It's not the only thing I have to confess. In the convent, we were forbidden to reveal our whole body, even when we were bathing. Here at the hotel, I took great pleasure in showering fully naked, and I felt exciting sensations in my body. I didn't even try to ignore them, even though one shouldn't give in to one's body.

I quickly change the subject and say, "It's unbelievable that the trip will be over tomorrow. What did you find particularly impressive?"

Suzy searches for words and replies, "The magnificent, tall structure of Notre Dame. The wonderful light penetrating through its huge stained-glass windows, together with the music, lifted my soul. I felt very close to God. And what captivated you, Rita?"

"The truth is, I don't have a preference. Everything we saw had a special and different beauty. It felt like a wonderful world was being revealed to me, which I got a small taste of and I want more. I sometimes feel like we're two little girls who might get lost when we go out into the world on our own. The convent suddenly seems too limiting to me. And the world is full of good Christians who aren't stuck in a convent, and life is good to them."

The pain at hearing this shows clearly on Suzy's face and I immediately regret speaking so openly. At the same time, this is also my delayed response to her criticism of how much I enjoyed the rich hotel food.

Volk's enthusiastic voice from beyond the door interrupts the tense conversation between us, "Are you ready to take a river cruise through the most beautiful city in the world?"

I'm excited. It's my first time on water, another first like so many other experiences we've had on this trip.

As with most of our sightseeing tours, Uncle Moshe won't be accompanying us this time either. I still think he doesn't feel comfortable with the bewildered eyes staring at us, a smartly dressed Jewish man with two cadet nuns wearing crosses.

Our long clothing makes it difficult for us to climb into the rocking boat, and my hem gets wet. There are seats along both sides of the boat. That way, on the way out we'll see one bank of the river, and the opposite bank on the way back. I grip the edge of the boat and try to surrender to the pleasant breeze. Suzy's sitting in front of me, and when I see how sad her face is I move to sit next to her and look for the right words to cheer her up.

It's hard to talk because we're being given an explanation in French over the loudspeaker of the sites we're seeing and the headset system for other languages is broken. Volk tries, with partial success, to overcome the loudspeaker and translate the information about the buildings, their names, the purpose they served in the past, and their purpose today.

I try to be nice to Suzy and say, "Look Suzy, it's so wonderful to be able to see the Eiffel Tower from everywhere, and look to the left, we're getting closer to Notre Dame. Now we can see it from the outside, which we couldn't on the day the rain took us by surprise. What a beautiful world God allows His believers to build."

Suzy nods her head in agreement and I hope she can feel how much I wish her well.

I share my impressions of the landscapes and places with Suzy and add, "I won't remember the names of most of these places…which of them is a train station that became a university, which the Musée d'Orsay or Sainte-Chapelle or the city hall, and I didn't even catch the name of so many others. I'm trying to take in all the sights and store them to memory. Suzy, I hope that you're enjoying it as much as I am."

Suzy gives me an appeasing smile and I feel relieved.

Behind the docks and along the entire bank, there are rows of trees and impressive buildings towering behind them. From time to time, we pass clusters of similar buildings with lots of rectangular windows, like eyes looking at us from above and saying, "You're just fleeting by while we have always been here, and here we'll remain."

We pass under the many bridges over the Seine that connect the two banks of the city. They're amazing in size and beauty. Each has its own name that I'm not going to list, other than the overly elaborate Pont Alexandre III with its golden statues. Now and then, we see ancient palaces along the bank and next to and behind them, beautiful, well-kept gardens. The banks are very wide and people are strolling along them and taking in all the beauty. Young couples are sitting and embracing on the banks of the river, which sparks forbidden jealousy in me.

Volk's voice cuts through the air, "The cruise is over and we'll walk back to the hotel. After dinner we'll rest and pack our luggage. Tomorrow morning the luggage will be transferred to the train for safekeeping and we'll say goodbye to the city with a bus tour around Paris. After that, we'll board the train."

Hearing these things, I feel the familiar sadness of painful farewells from the past and I turn to Suzy, "Suzy, did the trip end too soon for you too? I'm a little sad."

"To be honest," Suzy says. "I'm already tired. It was interesting but it's good that it's over. I miss the simple life I'm used to, the humble food, and the church near our house. Maybe I'm not suited to the abundance and pace of what we encountered. As to your question, if I'm sad that the trip is over, yes, a little. It's sad when things end knowing they won't be repeated."

After a short rest, we start packing. I debate whether to take the box of family photos and our documents in my carry-on bag or leave them in the luggage, which'll be waiting for us at the train station. Remembering how I lost my cardboard doll when we escaped from the train, makes me inclined to decide not to take them with me but to leave them in the luggage.

* * * *

It's our last night in Paris. Tomorrow night we'll be sailing the sea toward Antwerp and on our way home. Some incomprehensible sadness overwhelms me and I fall asleep without feeling joy at returning home.

A nightmare wakes me up in a panic. The luggage with our family photos drowns in the sea. Drenched in sweat and filled with anxiety, I rush to check my luggage. I find the documents, hold them to my heart, and sit on my bed. When I calm down, I look at the photos and remember longing for the good days before the decrees: a yellowed photo of Mama and Papa's wedding, and written on the back are all the names of the guests, all Mama's relatives. How beautiful she was. I recognize my grandfather. I loved him so much, and my grandmother and the uncle from Paris, Mama's brother.

The photo that moves me the most is of my fourth birthday party in my grandparents' beautiful home. I'm trying to blow out the candles in the chocolate cake, which was decorated with small, colorful candies, and everyone claps their hands. There's a photo showing me enthusiastically opening the gifts I received, with curious children, probably my cousins or friends of the family. A few days later, we were forced by order of the Nazis to move to another neighborhood, where the Jews of Berlin were concentrated. The memory hurts and brings tears to my eyes. I kneel in front of the picture of Mother Mary and Jesus that Suzy hung above our beds. I ask for forgiveness for my sins and whisper through my tears, "I want a family like I used to have."

Chapter 21

This morning we're saying goodbye to Paris, but first we'll take a bus tour and go passed all the beautiful and interesting places in the city, including the sites we didn't have a chance yet to visit. After the tour, we'll get on the train to the Port of Marseille and board the ship back to Antwerp. There, we'll say goodbye to Uncle Moshe and Volk, and then on our own, we'll continue to our home in the Netherlands near the border with Belgium.

Suzy is sitting next to me, and Volk and Uncle Moshe are sitting on a bench behind us. I have headphones on so I can listen to the explanations in German about the sites we're driving past. It's a wonderful way to say goodbye to the beautiful city.

I'm exhausted from the short and rough night I had, and every now and then I close my eyes and doze off. When we cross the bridge connecting the two parts of the city, the honking ship on the Seine wakes me up from a nightmare: Suzy and I are dressed as nuns and we're on the train back to our city. The train comes to a sudden stop, a gang of young men wearing brown uniforms who smell of fire chase us off the train to a place that's pure rubble. There's not a living soul in sight. We're terrified of the possibility that we won't be able to get out of there and return home, to our small apartment. "How will we manage to find our way home?" Suzy whimpers and drops to sit on the side of the destroyed road, and I raise my eyes to the sky and pray to Mother Mary to come and help us. Out of the corner of my eye, I see a church.

Suzy speaks from my choking throat, "Mother Mary's answered my prayers. Look, there's a small church in front of us, let's walk there."

The road is full of potholes and it's difficult to pass. Sometimes it feels like we're getting no closer…another hill…another valley, but we're determined to make it there.

We're there. Silence. The church is deserted. A picture of the Madonna with Jesus is hanging loosely on the wall. We kneel before it, cross ourselves, and start to cry. Where will our salvation come from?

Volk's voice announcing that the tour is over interrupts the terrifying dream, and while I'm recovering, I wonder what the dream means.

"We've arrived," Volk says again, interrupting my thoughts.

We walk toward the train station and at the entrance Volk takes out a camera from his stuffed knapsack and takes a picture of me and Suzy.

I'm surprised. "I didn't know you had a camera," I say. "Why only now, at the last minute?"

"I don't like using my camera when I'm traveling," Volk replies. "When I do, I don't enjoy the view because I'm focused on taking pictures. We'll buy a few postcards at the train station, memorabilia to remind you of the places you've seen. They're more beautiful than any pictures I could take. I've taken one of you now so that you'll have proof that you were here."

Uncle Moshe rushes us to our designated carriage on the train. I realize that he's been urging us all day not to be late, even this morning. I ask Volk why Uncle Moshe is under so much pressure and he replies that we have to board the ship before the Sabbath begins because today is Friday, and if Heaven forbid we miss the train, we'll have to stay in Paris and our whole schedule will be off. Then we'd have to change the date for the ship.

"Why is it so important to arrive before the Sabbath begins?" I ask. "And how does he know when it does begin?"

"I'll explain it to you later, when we're on the train."

While we're boarding, Suzy glares at me, "Why are you so interested in Jewish customs?"

I reply with a smile to hide that I don't like her question, "Oh really, Suzy, you have nothing to worry about my faith. I've always been curious and I've always asked questions. I'm sure you remember me telling you how the priest who prepared me for communion praised me for it."

The train carriage is spacious and comfortable and it's exclusively ours. Volk takes sandwiches and bottles of water out of his knapsack and places them on the table. The sandwiches bear the name of the hotel we were staying at. He invites us to eat our late lunch. This is the first time since the beginning of the trip that Uncle Moshe is eating with us.

Although we didn't eat a thing in the morning, Suzy declares that she's not hungry and that she prefers to rest. I realize that she's angry and worried. She's been reacting this way since we first met that uncle of ours from Paris and she learned that she was born Jewish.

We each whisper our own prayer before we eat and then fall silent. Volk is the first to break the silence when he turns to me and says, "Now I'll answer your question about the Sabbath, which is the heart of Judaism: God finished creating the world before the seventh day, and then He stopped. The Hebrew word for Sabbath—Shabbat—means 'stopped work.' In other words, He finished His creation and sanctified the Sabbath, the stopping of work. The fourth of the Ten Commandments requires the people of Israel to keep the Sabbath as a covenant with God. That's why it's so important and must be kept faithfully. There's a belief that says if all the people of Israel keep the Sabbath, the Messiah will come. As for your second question, the Sabbath begins on Friday at sunset and all work and everything relating to it has to stop."

Suzy, who's pretending not to listen, mutters to herself, "What, traveling by train is work but sailing on a ship isn't? The Messiah doesn't set conditions in order to appear—Jesus wants to save and help us unconditionally."

Volk ignores what she says, or perhaps he doesn't hear her.

I sink into very hazy memories of Friday evenings at my grandparents, when my grandmother would light two candles, cover her face with both hands, and mumble a blessing in a language I didn't understand, but I remember being enthralled by the candlelight and its dwindling length. My grandfather would pour wine and say a blessing. I loved the sweet desserts we ended the meal with. But other, terrifying memories arise, from those days—of breaking glass, of the Nazi youth battalions in brown uniforms that I'd encounter on my way to school. They'd shout, "1,2,3, *Yuden Raus* (Jews out);" Memories of worrying if Papa would make it home safely, of the lack of food because Papa had lost his job, of the train trip to Belgium on our own, of being deported at night and stuffed into a train crowded with frightened people.

My memory of the fear is real and not hazy. It penetrated every cell in my body, it followed me throughout all the years of my life in the convent. I was afraid that people would find out that I'm Jewish, afraid of the German soldiers in the convent.... The years of fear are an inseparable part of my emotions. I'm still hiding my Jewish origins under my nun's uniform and the large cross that hangs over it. Suzy never experienced this fear in the convent. On the contrary, her fears are from the postwar period and are different from mine. Hers are in the present. She's afraid that the Jews are going to kidnap her.

After we eat lunch, I look out the open window at the passing landscape and bask in the pleasant breeze on my face until the tiredness takes over and my eyes close. Then I spend the rest of the train ride dozing uneasily.

We've arrived. Uncle Moshe breathes a sigh of relief, we got there on time. We board the ship with all our belongings an hour before we set sail, and get ready for a trip of a few days in a two-cabin suite with a common dining area just for us.

Suzy hangs up her picture of Mother Mary and Jesus, kneels, and crosses herself. I do the same.

There's a knock on the door. Volk asks, "Do you want to join us in welcoming the Sabbath? We'll light the candles and then eat the Sabbath meal."

Suzy shakes her head vigorously at me. She doesn't want to and I pass on her message.

"That's fine," Volk replies. "We'll have your meal sent to your cabin."

Chapter 22

After the tiring day we had yesterday, we go to bed early. A pale light coming through the window wakes me up early in the morning from a deep, dreamless sleep. For a few seconds I wonder where I am until I remember that I'm on the ship on my way home. The trip will be over soon. Suzy's still sleeping peacefully. I surrender to the pleasant rocking of the ship and doze off again to get a full night's sleep. There's no reason to jump out of bed. I don't remember when I had a real day off, a day without having to get up for work or to do anything at all. I feel a slight twinge of pain knowing that there are no days off like these waiting for us back home.

I look around the small cabin. It's furniture is unremarkable. I pause at the window, which is calling me to peek out and see what's beyond. I stretch with pleasure and slowly stretch out one foot at a time to a small bedside rug on the bare wooden floor. I kneel by the bed facing the picture of the Holy Mother with Jesus in her lap, which Suzy immediately hung up yesterday when we arrived. I pray for a safe journey, cross myself, and walk barefoot to the window. The window reveals an infinite, quiet blue sea that meets the skyline and together they form a circular shell that appears to block any way out and beyond it. I shiver. There's something terrifying about how infinite the water is, but the soothing light of the sun's first rays are radiating from somewhere.

I hear Volk's voice through the door, "Breakfast's waiting for us in the dining area."

Suzy wakes up and after saying her morning prayers and washing, we go for breakfast.

Uncle Moshe and Volk are already waiting for us. They greet us with a smile and wish us Shabbat Shalom in Hebrew. There's no longer any need to translate the words for us. Volk translates the prayer that Uncle Moshe recites before the meal, thanking God, the King of the world, who brings forth bread from the earth. Suzy and I also offer our prayer of thanks to God, thanking Him for the food on our table. The clinking of dishes is grating against the silence.

I squint at Suzy and notice that she's devoured a whole slice of bread and half a glass of orange juice. This cheers me up and I break the silence with a comment that I immediately regret, "There's no difference between our blessings on the food and yours. In both, we thank the same God for providing the food that we've received."

Afraid of Suzy's reaction, I'm surprised when she says pleasantly and out of character, "The difference between us is that God sent his son our Savior, Jesus, to save us, while you're waiting for the Messiah who's taking his time and hasn't come to save you yet."

I nod my head in agreement, curious to hear Uncle Moshe's response. Volk answers in his place, "If all the Jews keep the Sabbath, the Messiah will come to save them."

I've heard similar things from Uncle Moshe, who interrupts the conversation with a proposal, "Rita, I have a suggestion for you. After we finish eating, take out the family photos and documents that your father left with the Mother Superior. You can both get to know your family through the stories I can tell you about each of them, about the few who were saved and the many who were not."

I take out the bundle of photos that my father gave the Mother Superior, the photos she hid in the iron box deep in the hole in the church altar.

My hands are shaking as I spread them out on the dining room table. Uncle Moshe's moved but tries to hide it. He leans over the photos and picks up a group photograph from his wedding. It was soon after the First World War ended. The words on the back are in Polish and are illegible, but Uncle Moshe remembers exactly what it says and the date of his wedding, of course.

"These are your grandparents from Poland," he says, his voice cracking, and he points at a man with a beard, sidelocks, and a black hat. A full woman is standing beside him with an old-fashioned hat on her head. They look very different from my German grandparents. I saw Jews like them when the Germans forced us to leave our home and concentrated us in an overcrowded, squalid part of Berlin.

Uncle Moshe tries to hide his tears as he strokes the photo of his dead wife.

Volk translates for him, "These are all seven of my siblings, all younger than me. Do you recognize your father?"

I jump for joy when I recognize Papa. "He's the young boy with short sidelocks and a skullcap on his head!"

Suzy shifts uncomfortably when she looks at the photo. There's no denying her Jewish origin anymore, it's blatantly clear what her ancestors look like.

Uncle Moshe continues telling us about them all. "This is the rebel, my brother who left the faith, volunteered to fight in the Spanish Civil War and never returned...and this is Uncle Dov, who moved to Israel with your grandparents before the Second World War. He has a son a few years younger than Suzy. By the way, they sent you their regards and they hope to meet you someday."

Uncle Moshe sighs and adds in Yiddish, "Everyone else in the photo didn't survive—all four of my other siblings, your father, our uncles and aunts, our cousins. The Lord will avenge their blood."

Suzy whispers in my ear, "If the God of the Jews can avenge their blood, then why didn't he prevent their death?"

Chapter 23

Looking at the family photos was very emotional for us, and we eat lunch together in silence. Everyone is immersed in their own thoughts.

Suzy, whose appetite is improving slightly, is still weak, and she decides to rest in our cabin. Before Uncle Moshe retires for his regular afternoon rest, I ask Volk if we can go up to the deck for a breath of fresh air. Volk asks Uncle Moshe if it's all right, but Uncle Moshe shakes his finger no, he won't allow it, and adds that after dinner, after the sun sets, we'll all go. I return disappointed to my cabin and wonder why he refused. Why don't we go up to the deck during the day when there's still light? Is he hiding us? Is he ashamed of us?

In our room, I rummage through the dresser drawers. I find stationery, and decide to write about our trip to the Mother Superior. While I'm weighing how to start the letter, I see that at the top of each page there's a blue symbol that resembles the Hebrew letter Shin. I remember it from the little Hebrew that I learned in the few months I spent at the Jewish school in Belgium. During dinner, I tell them about it. Volk looks questioningly at Uncle Moshe, who after a few seconds' hesitation, answers that there really is a similarity, but it's an ancient Greek letter because the ship is owned by a Greek company.

* * * *

In the evening we go up to the deck. It's a clear night without a cloud in the sky and I take relieving breaths of fresh air. They're intoxicating after being stuck in our cabin for two days. The length and breadth of the sky is endless and its packed full of countless stars. I don't think I've ever seen such a huge sky. We could see only a slice of it from the convent windows, and we never went outside at night...we always went to bed early.

Cheerful singing suddenly erupts from the lower decks. Uncle Moshe explains that they're migrant workers from North Africa who are traveling as a group to look for a living in the Low Countries, and that it's better not to run into them.

* * * *

After breakfast on our third day at sea, Volk surprises us by spilling dozens of pieces of illustrated cardboard cut into different shapes onto the dining table. We have to put them together and form the picture on the back of the box. The picture is of Notre-Dame Cathedral. I've never seen this kind of game before, and I enjoy it so much that I ask to eat in our cabin so that we don't have to take apart the pieces that we've already matched up and put together. After lunch, only Volk, Suzy, and I continue the fun activity.

While we're searching for matching pieces, Volk surprises me and Suzy with a question, "In two-days' time, our voyage at sea will end. I assume that Rita will be going back to work in the laboratory. What about you, Suzy? You haven't turned fifteen yet."

Suzy immediately answers, "I'll look for a job, and when I'm eighteen I'll join a church and become a nun."

"You know," Volk replies. "There are Catholic monasteries in Israel, and a few convents for women. Monks, nuns, and Christians make pilgrimages to Israel from all over the world. They join organized tour groups to visit the holy Christian sites, where Jesus lived and worked, such as the Church of the Holy

Sepulchre in Jerusalem, where he was crucified, buried, and resurrected. They visit the Sea of Galilee, where he performed the miracle of walking on water, and many other places, where he spread his teachings."

"I'm impressed, you know a lot about Christianity," Suzy responds sarcastically.

"That's right, and I hope that someday you'll also come visit and meet your family. And what about you Rita, what are your plans?"

"Like Suzy, I also thought about becoming a nun, but when I brought it up with the Mother Superior, she said that before I take such a significant step, I should also get to know normal life outside the convent, after spending so many years there. That's why she arranged the job in the laboratory for me. In the meantime, I'm going back to my previous everyday life. Time will tell which direction I choose to go in."

I don't dare to tell Suzy that lately I've started longing for a family of my own, and that the trip to Paris only made this need in me stronger. Despite being slightly afraid of Uncle Moshe, I do feel that he's taking the place of a caring father.

We finish putting all the pieces of the puzzle together and the picture of Notre-Dame Cathedral is complete. What a shame that we have to take it apart and put the pieces back in the box.

Volk surprises me, "I see that you really like the puzzle. It's my gift to you."

Happy, I thank him.

Just before evening, Suzy and I start to feel unwell. The sea is rough, the waves are high, and the ship is starting to rock harder. Suzy feels nauseous and stops eating, and Volk explains that it's common in this area. Soon, in a day we'll reach land and everything will be fine.

* * * *

This morning is our last on the ship. The sea is calm again, the sun is bright and warm, and we pack our things and prepare to go ashore. We look out into the distance and wait to see land as soon as it appears.

"I can see land, I can see land." Suzy jumps for joy. "But I wonder what that mountain is, getting taller as we get closer. Since when is there a mountain so close to the Port of Antwerp? It's in the Low Countries. And never in my life have I been blinded by such strong sunlight. Where are we?!"

My whole body convulses as I have the terrible feeling that a bad prophecy is coming true. Did Suzy see it coming? Have we been misled and kidnapped by the Jews, by our Jewish uncle, our father's brother, our own flesh and blood?

The honks of the ship entering the port hit me in the head. Suzy's standing next to me, she still doesn't understand where we are. I grab her hand and tell her, "Something's worrying me, look at that group of youngsters. Uncle Moshe said they that they're from North Africa and that they're looking for work. They look like us. Can you also hear them? And they're speaking German and Yiddish."

Suzy turns pale and I grab her hand and say, "Hold on. I need to find out what's going on. Tell Volk I forgot something in the cabin. Wait for me until I get back."

I approach a group of cheerful youth. They're singing as they pass me by. A girl smiles at me and says in German, "We're finally here, in our own country, the Land of Israel."

Her friend answers her, "Shh...that's one of the two Jewish girls who grew up in the convent. We're not allowed to have contact with them because they have no idea that they're going to Israel."

I'm stunned into silence. My stomach turns and I return to Suzy and Volk, who literally pushes us toward the bridge to the dock, and the look on my face conveys the terrible news to Suzy. We've been deceived and kidnapped.

Uncle Moshe is waiting for us when we step onto the dock, and Suzy screams at him, "You deceitful Jew, you kidnapped us!" She walks up to him, her eyes terrified and her fists up. Volk grabs her arms before she can hit him and she collapses into heartbreaking sobs on the dock.

Chapter 24

I help Volk to lead Suzy to the cab that'll take us to Tel Aviv. He says goodbye to us and rushes off to his family, who are waiting for him on the dock.

Suzy curls up in the back seat of the cab. Her head is resting on my lap. I can feel the tension in her body, and every now and then, a weak sob escapes her. I stroke her face and steal a glance at Uncle Moshe's tormented face in the mirror. He's sitting in the front. I try not to be moved by his expression, and I fight with myself to hate him. I can't, even though he'd intentionally deceived us and lied to us.

He doesn't utter a word on the way. The only sound other than Suzy's sobs is the noise of the engine. The blue sea and white foam appear and disappear. I recall the signs in Uncle Moshe's behavior, signs that in my innocence I didn't notice... he prevented us from going on deck...he made sure that we ate all our meals in the cabin so that we wouldn't run into the youth group on their way to Israel. We didn't see the sunlight at all during the trip. He lied when he told me that the Hebrew letter "Shin" on the letterhead was a Greek letter, and I naively accepted his explanation without question. Realizing how he deceived, I have mixed feelings. There is such immense rage in me that if I'd had the courage, I would have punched him like Suzy intended to. I feel so insulted by his exploitation of our innocence, such pain that he didn't take our feelings into consideration, nor take into account the damage his actions would cause Suzy. At the same time, I wonder about the source of his deep determination and desire to bring us into his family, to take the place of the father we lost, and to spend so much money planning and executing such a complex scheme. He's so different from our French uncle, my mother's brother. He gave up so easily, and had no intention of opening up his home in France to us. He didn't even try to convince us to join the organization that was gathering surviving Jewish children without parents in Belgium. Despite my anger, to my surprise I feel like this is the first time I'm in a place that welcomes me, a place where I don't have to hide my Jewish origin.

* * * *

We're staying at Uncle Moshe's home. He has a double-story house surrounded by a garden that's shaded by trees. Uncle Moshe's wife, Aunt Hela, speaks German and she receives us with polite kindness and no hugs. She's a tall, very attractive woman, her eyes are dark brown, big, and intelligent, and she seems to be in her fifties. Her light brown hair peeks out from the elegant headscarf that she's wrapped around her hair to cover it. Her long, loose dress matches the headscarf, and I notice her fresh, light scent.

She shows us to our room on the first floor. I hold Suzy up until we get to the room. It has two beds, and she collapses onto the first. Aunt Hela disappears and quickly returns with a woman holding bed linen and nightgowns. The woman is the maid (and maid is the first word I learn in Hebrew in Israel) and she makes up the other bed for sleeping, even though it's the middle of the day. Aunt Hela asks me in German to change Suzy from her nun's habit into a nightgown, and to help her into bed. She adds that she'll give us some time to ourselves and the maid will bring us water, orange juice, and cookies.

"See you at dinner," she says firmly before closing the door behind us.

Suzy is lying with her pale face to the wall. Her body is curled into a ball as if it wants to limit its contact with the reality it's so uncomfortable with. I can barely persuade her to drink some water. I kneel by her bed, hold her skinny hand, and with my free hand I cross myself and pray to the Holy Mother to watch over her and give her the strength to overcome the injustice and the trauma she's in at being in the very situation she was so afraid of.

I drink the juice, eat a few cookies, and look around. The room is tastefully furnished and feels light and calming. There's plenty of light coming from the big window. The curtains match the bedcovers, and there's a bedside cabinet by each bed. I notice the round table, chairs, and a two-door closet on the opposite wall. They're all made of sparkling clean pale wood. Feeling helpless, I rest my head on my hands and wonder what the future holds for us. It's not the first time that my life has been turned upside down and I allow myself some release and burst into painful tears.

Suzy refuses to join me for dinner in "my family's" spacious dining room, and she stays in the bedroom. The maid serves the meal and we each bless the food according to our own faith. The aroma of the food and sitting together remind me of the cozy home atmosphere I was denied for all those years. Aunt Hela apologizes that the meal is modest because the war's just ended and food is being rationed. I learn the word *omelet* and that the food in a jar that resembles cream is called *lebben*. We eat in silence until suddenly Uncle Moshe puts down his cutlery and wipes his mouth with his white napkin. We each have one. His hands are shaking, and for a moment he covers his face before turning hesitantly to me.

Aunt Hela translates his words into German, "Rita, believe me, Suzy's condition worries me very much. I take responsibility for it and I'm trying to find a way to ease her distress and gain her trust that I have no intention of tearing you away from your faith."

He pauses for a second and continues, "What do you think about me taking you to prayers at the Catholic church in Jaffa? Maybe that'll cheer her up and she'll understand that she'll need to build up her physical strength for that. Please tell her about my offer."

I don't answer him. Without making a sound, I think to myself, More than easing Suzy's distress, you want to ease your own conscience. I need to grab this moment.

I feel a glimmer of hope and I answer in German, "I like the idea. I'll try to get through to her."

When we finish eating, I return to the room, stroke Suzy's face, and smile. With forced happiness, I say, "Our prayers have borne fruit, our Holy Mother Mary has opened our uncle's closed heart. He understands now that he has to compromise with us. He asked if he can accompany us to the church in Jaffa as soon as you can stand firmly on your feet."

Suzy turns her gray face to me and hisses, "I don't believe a word that man says and I'll never forgive him."

Chapter 25

Two days have passed since we arrived in Israel, and Suzy is still lying with her face to the wall and refusing to eat.

The maid knocks lightly on the door. She has a tray of food for Suzy, which she sets down on the table.

"Suzy," I say pleadingly as I take her hand. "We're not here out of choice, but at the moment we can't leave. Even if Uncle Moshe doesn't keep his promise to take us to the church, you and I will find a way to get there, but only on condition that you stop punishing yourself for something that's not your fault. Please eat what they call lebben and a little bread. The spread isn't real butter but it's quite similar. I need you, don't get lost on me."

Suzy finally relents, makes peace with a small portion of food, but not with herself or with her situation. Her gaze is frozen and she's still withdrawn. From time to time she snaps out of it, talks to herself, and asks without expecting an answer, "Who am I? Christian? Jewish? I don't want to be Jewish, even if I was born one. My body's not important, my soul is connected to God and Jesus Christ. When are we going to church?" And then she disappears into her shell again.

* * * *

A few more days pass before she's prepared to leave the room and go out to the terrace that looks out into the garden.

Summer's here early. It's so hot. At the end of the day, we slowly and silently sip fresh orange juice on the shady terrace. The soft light of dusk is bursting through the branches of the trees, and a cool wind is stirring the leaves and gliding pleasantly over my face, dulling the humid heat. A feeling of peace and calm washes over me. The remnants of fear of my Jewish origin being revealed, a fear that's always been part of my life and that didn't dissipate even after the war, is beginning to fade now.

I wonder if Uncle Moshe will keep his promise to accompany us to church. That'll be a real test for him. I don't share my thoughts with Suzy.

The maid calls us for dinner. As she's still refusing to eat with us, I see Suzy to our room and we find long thin dresses that are suitable for the summer heat. Someone's taking care of us, I think to myself. We'll wear our convent clothes only when we go out.

It's not the only surprise today. During dinner, Aunt Hela informs me that Uncle Moshe will take us to Sunday Mass at the church in Jaffa, and says, "The city of Jaffa is under military rule because it's an Arab city and one needs a permit to visit. Uncle Moshe made a lot of effort to receive permission from the military authorities to bring you to pray in the church, as it's in Jaffa. He'll wait in the church's courtyard until you're done."

I thank Uncle Moshe, and I can't stop smiling with gratitude even though the anger I feel at him for deceiving us hasn't faded. I rush off to tell Suzy the news.

At the news, a glimmer of light flashes in Suzy's eyes. She hugs me really hard, and with great effort tries to eat the dinner I brought her. She even partially succeeds.

* * * *

It's the morning we've been waiting for. Dressed in our convent clothes, with our crucifixes displayed prominently on our chests, we walk with Uncle Moshe through the city streets. It's a regular weekday, but for us it's our special Sunday. It's the first time since we arrived that we've gone out into the city. A few people smile at us, but most of them look in wonder at the religious Jewish man with the beard, striking in his appearance, who's walking along with two girls wearing large crucifixes.

We can see the church in the distance. It's on the top of a hill. Its façade is brown and white and palm trees tower around it.

In eager anticipation, we get there and stop in an area surrounded by a barbed wire fence, evidence of the war that was just here. A soldier in uniform stops us. His eyes widen in amazement at the sight of such a strange trio. Uncle Moshe hands him our entry permit. The soldier allows us to enter while uttering a few words to Uncle Moshe, who responds with a forgiving smile. I don't understand what he says but I can feel that it was about our appearance. Uncle Moshe sits in the courtyard in the shade of a tree and waits there until Mass is over.

A tremor of emotion grips me as I enter the big, magnificent church with its supporting pillars and pink marble walls decorated with oil paintings depicting the stations along Christ's tormenting path. I notice the stained glass on both sides of the rounded ceiling. I'm filled with a feeling of holiness. I feel around for Suzy's hand, and we both kneel and cross ourselves. There are only a few people praying in the church. Mass begins. The smell of the incense, the sounds of the organ, the singing of the choir that always cast a spell on me, and the sensation that God is here, take me back to the old days, to a place where I belonged for so many years; a place that gave me a sense of security that Jesus and Mother Mary are watching over me. My thoughts distract me from the priest's sermon and I find myself wondering: Have all the recent events been a confusing dream of feeling betrayed by my father's brother mixed with a longing for a family? A longing for a family that'll take care of me even though their faith is different from mine, a family that at the same time painfully reminds me of my parents and my childhood home?

When Mass is over, I lead Suzy to the confession booth. I badly need to ask the priest's forgiveness for the confusion I'm feeling.

"Pray, my daughter," the priest answers me. "Prayers will help you follow your heart."

I join Uncle Moshe outside in the courtyard while muttering to myself, "But I'm torn inside."

Suzy comes out, and I can see on her face that she feels better now that she's confessed. She sits beside me in a world of her own.

In silence, we look out from the courtyard on top of the hill. It's surrounded by a tranquil green garden. I look at where the magical blue sea meets the Jaffa harbor's sand dunes that are illuminated by the golden sunlight. As the scene unfolds before me, my former residence feels gray and faded.

Surprised, I ask myself if I could, would I want to go back?

Chapter 26

A few days later at dinner (without Suzy, who was still refusing to join us), after we each silently said our own faith's version of the blessing of the food, I notice that my uncle is staring at his plate. Aunt Hela looks hesitant. The tension in the air is palpable.

Uncharacteristically, she looks questioningly at him, as if asking for confirmation of what she's about to say. "Rita, it's been a week since you arrived," she begins. "It's time to discuss the rest of your life in Israel. We're happy to have you stay with us here, but as you know, your uncle is the rabbi of a community. Unfortunately, the people of the community haven't taken kindly to the crucifixes you wear in his home, so we'll have to find you other accommodation."

My aunt takes a deep breath, as if relieved that the task is behind her, while my breath catches and my heart skips a beat. I feel as if I've been shot with an arrow, straight into a wound that's still not completely healed, reawakening an old familiar pain from the past—the pain of being rejected as a Jew. And now I'm being rejected as a Christian.... Will I now have to hide my belief in Jesus, just like once I had to hide my Jewish origin?

"You know," she adds in a voice that makes it clear how difficult this is for her. "You have more family here in Tel Aviv. They came to see you at the port, but you didn't actually get to meet them. We'll have a get-together, here at our place, and decide together on you future path—where you'll live, which school would suit Suzy. It's important that you both learn Hebrew. Rita, we're asking you what you want to do because you're already an adult."

I'm dumbstruck. I don't have the strength and maybe the courage to share with my relatives the pain they've caused me. In any case, would there be any point in telling them?

We finish the meal in silence, avoiding each other's eyes. When we're done, I stand up, and on my way out, I say almost in a whisper and with a hint of defiance, "I'll pray to my God that Suzy and I will find the right way for us to stay in this place, which we were brought to under false pretenses and against our will."

I'm in no hurry to get back to our room. I sit down on a bench on the terrace. It's illuminated by the soft light of the moon. I try to calm the flurry of emotions and I wonder what kind of place we'll be sent to. Will it be as elegant as Uncle Moshe's house? Will our other aunt be less regal than Aunt Hela, and more motherly?

It gets cold and I go to our room. Suzy's sleeping, curled up like a snail. I'm afraid of her reaction to the news. I don't know how she'll react. I'm tired. I don't have the mental strength to deal with her too. In the meantime, I'll let her—and myself—be. I look at the beautiful, well-kept room. An old, painful sorrow spreads through my body, a pain that reminds me of so many goodbyes from the places that we've had to leave.

Just like on other days, before I go to bed, I kneel down, pray, and ask Mother Mary to show me the path to take; to show me how to keep my faith while I'm being held captive by my relatives, who although they want what's best for me, their ways aren't mine.

I toss and turn all night. As I doze, images from the past appear before me. Papa telling me when he handed us over to the convent that I shouldn't forget that I'm Jewish and that I shouldn't tell Suzy because she's too young to keep a secret...the image of the Mother Superior telling me, after several meetings with Uncle Moshe, that Suzy and I belong with the Jewish people and that we should live among them...that family is very important, especially a family that sees us as part of its people. The Mother Superior added then that people have freedom of religion in Israel, and convents. In my dream, I hear Uncle Moshe saying during one of our meetings at the convent that Suzy and I were born Jewish and there's no way to change that, but he also reassured us by adding that a person cannot be made to forget their faith unless they want to and choose to.

I wake up with a thought that won't budge: Did the Mother Superior see this coming? Did she collaborate with Uncle Moshe? I'll never know, but maybe in this way, through the memories surfacing in a dream, she's helping me find my way. I have a growing sense that we have to come to terms with the fact that we're Jewish by birth, while at the same time we believe in Jesus. Suddenly everything becomes clear despite the pain. Yes, that'll be my way to survive because I want a life.

It's going to be difficult to convey this to Suzy.

Suzy insistently refuses to come meet the family. She holds her hands over her ears, like a spoiled child. I try to persuade her by telling her that we have no other solution but to come to terms with the fact that we were born to Jewish parents, that before Papa left us in the convent, he tried to send us to Israel and failed because we were too young.

I tell her that when Papa left us at the convent, he asked me not to forget that I'm Jewish, and that Jesus was also a Jew by birth, and as such, she can continue to put her faith in Him. I try to explain to her that she's still a minor, and until she reaches adulthood, she'll have to accept that even though by law she doesn't have control over her daily life, she does have control over her faith.

Despite all my pleas and explanations, she digs her heels in and refuses to attend the family get-together because she hasn't forgiven Uncle Moshe, and nor will she ever. That's when I run out of patience. I raise my voice and more furious at her than I've ever been, I say, "You're not as true a Christian as you think you are! Jesus commanded us to forgive even our enemies; to turn the other cheek to those who hurt us! For the sake of your faith, you must see to it that you reach maturity and then you can fulfill your vocation as a nun, even here in Israel."

Chapter 27

It's a hot summer weekday afternoon, and we're waiting to meet our uncle and his wife and son for the first time. Suzy and I are wearing our convent uniform and our crucifixes around our necks. Uncle Moshe and Aunt Hela are dressed in fine clothes and are their usual restrained selves. We hear the doorbell alerting us that they've arrived, and then the sound of their footsteps on the path leading to the front door as it opens.

For a moment, a burst of sadness chokes me: The man standing in the doorway looks so much like Papa, only his body is fuller. The man doesn't give my mind time to dwell on the memory because as he walks in he comes straight toward me with his hand extended and says in Yiddish, "*Ich bin Dov, daina tattes kleine broeder.*" (I'm Dov, your father's younger brother.) I extend my hand to shake his, smile, and nod to say I understand what he's saying. He rests his hand on his wife's shoulder. "*Das ist mein weif Rachel.*" (This is my wife, Rachel.) Pointing at the boy, he adds, "*Das ist mein son, Gadi.*" (This is my son, Gadi.)

He turns to Suzy and she responds to his outstretched hand with a limp hand and a sealed face, as if the devil himself is forcing her to.

Aunt Rachel comes up and hugs me warmly. The smell of her full, sweaty body after walking here in the middle of summer is unpleasant, but I overcome my resistance and surrender to her hug, moved by her surprising show of affection. From the look on her face, Suzy's clearly uncomfortable with the hug she's next in line for.

We're invited out to the spacious terrace. It's rounded edges meet the green summer grass, which has started to fade in the summer sun. Light steam is rising from the grass, which has just been watered in order to freshen up the air a little and infuse it with its special smell. On the terrace, there are two benches and a few wicker chairs with pretty, colorful cushions on them. Glass jars of cold drinks are already on the small tables, ready to refresh us from the last of the summer heat.

Our cousin, Gadi, who looks a few years younger than Suzy, hops eagerly to the terrace and asks his father, pointing at us, "Abba, tell me, are they goys?"

I understand what he's saying even though he's speaking in Hebrew. After all, I did learn Hebrew for a short while when I attended the Jewish school in Belgium, and I heard the word goy more than once.

"Shh..." Aunt Rachel scolds him. "It's not polite to talk like that. I already told you that they're Jewish but they grew up in a convent so they could be saved from the Nazis, and they're your cousins."

I understand the content of her words from her reproachful tone, and I sneak a forgiving smile at him.

Uncle Dov speaks to us in Yiddish as he points at his clothes. From what I understand, he's apologizing for the way he's dressed because he came straight from work. I nod my head in understanding and say to myself that it looks like I'm going to improve my Yiddish faster than my Hebrew.

Suzy shows no interest, she's detached, withdrawn, and in her own world. Her head is hanging and her fingers are clenched into fists and cutting into her flesh. I feel her pain. She doesn't belong here, and she's longing for her old life back. I hope she comes to her senses and holds on until she reaches adulthood and then chooses her own path.

Aunt Hela interrupts my thoughts and explains in German, "Uncle Dov and Aunt Rachel have a kiosk, which is a small store that's open to the street. They sell newspapers, confectionary, drinks, and sandwiches to passersby."

I notice that despite how similar the appearance of the two brothers is, they seem to have very different personalities. Uncle Dov and Aunt Rachel are tanned from the strong Israeli sun, their hands are rough from work, and their bodies are full. They're not elegant like our hosts are, but on the other hand they radiate more kindness. Uncle Dov doesn't have a beard, his hair is short, and he's wearing a small black yarmulke that looks brand new, as if he's wearing it for the first time and in honor of his rabbi brother. His wife Rachel's hair isn't covered, and she's not wearing any make-up. Her face isn't distinctive, her dress doesn't indicate good taste, and she's wearing flat, worn-out work shoes.

For a brief moment, no one says anything until Aunt Hela, with her sharp senses, signals to the maid who's waiting in the corner to open the living room doors and invite us in to eat. A selection of delicacies are waiting for us on the fancy sideboard, which has been covered with a festive tablecloth: cold drinks, tiny sandwiches, colorful salads, tempting cookies, chocolates... an abundance that's completely inappropriate for the period of austerity we're currently in. Suzy and I stay seated. The first to respond to the invitation is Gadi, who enthusiastically piles his plate high until his mother stops him and whispers something in his ear. He puts down his heavy plate, smiles, and brings me and Suzy some refreshments.

All of us dig in, except Suzy of course, and only the sound of us rummaging around in our plates disturbs the silence.

Finally, Uncle Moshe stands up, says a few words in Hebrew, looks at Aunt Hela, and she—turning to me and Suzy—says in German, "We're gathered here to celebrate Rita and Suzy's joining our family and we'd like to help them adjust and feel part of the people they belong to."

I don't look at Suzy sitting next to me but I can still feel the angry spasm running through her body.

Our aunt continues, "You'll have to learn Hebrew. In a few days, the school summer vacation begins and it lasts for two months. It's time for us to organize a Hebrew study group for you. Gadi will happily walk there and back with you, and as soon as the school year begins, we'll find a suitable school for Suzy, and Rita will decide what profession she wants to work in. You're going to stay with Uncle Dov and Aunt Rachel."

Her words are met with silence. I can feel a burning sense of indignity growing in me. They've never asked what I want to do with my life. Maybe I'd prefer to finish school? My relatives don't see me as mature enough. They think I need supervision and someone to make sure I find my way, or could they be afraid that Suzy and I will run away? They don't understand that we're trapped, we're in their hands. Still, we may physically be captives but we're free in our faith.

I don't have the words or the courage and inner strength I once had to express my feelings and respond. Am I afraid of Uncle Moshe's reaction, because I rely on him for my physical existence?

I'm a prisoner of predetermined decisions, I have no choice of my own, and the worst of all, I don't have the tools to change it.

Suddenly Suzy raises her bowed head, breaks the silence with a kind of tranquil outburst, and says in her gentle voice as she turns her gaze on Uncle Moshe. Aunt Hela translates for her, "I ask and hope that you'll keep your promise and allow us to attend church every Sunday and on our holidays."

Surprised, Uncle Moshe clears his throat, says, "Ja." He nods his head to signal to his wife, who expands his answer in German. "Uncle Moshe will continue to accompany you on Sundays to church in Jaffa, and on the days when he can't, Aunt Rachel will take his place."

I note to myself that he'd prepared his answer in advance, but if it weren't for Suzy's courage to ask, he wouldn't have brought it up.

Chapter 28

At the end of the day, the family get-together draws to a close and we pack our belongings in our parting gift from Uncle Moshe: two new knapsacks to replace the worn suitcases we arrived with in Israel. As we're leaving, I extend my hand to Uncle Moshe, who shakes my hand warmly.

"My dear uncle and aunt," I say. "On behalf of Suzy and myself, I'd like to say thank you for your hospitality and dedicated care."

I think his eyes are moist when Aunt Hela translates his reply, "I'll meet you next Sunday on your way to church and I'll always be here for you in place of the father you lost. I hope that soon we'll be able to converse in Hebrew and understand each other better, because you're very important to me."

Aunt Hela takes a step toward me and kisses my cheek for the first time.

Suzy, her face hard, rushes past us and before walking out the door, she says, "*Danke furseine gastfreundshcaftdt.*" (I thank you for your hospitality.)

New times are ahead for us. We're on our way to another station in our lives.

We walk with our new family toward our new residence. The street lights come on and compete with the light from the full moon. We all sink into silence, which is violated only by the roar of passing cars. I'm lost in thought, recalling Uncle Moshe's parting words, which managed to touch me and soften the pain he's caused us. Can I ever forgive him? Is my anger over being deceived beginning to dull? Is the anger giving way to an understanding that his deceitful act stemmed from a deep sense of mission? I suddenly appreciate the great effort it took for Uncle Moshe to bring us back into the bosom of his people when he's convinced that they're our people and that only in Israel do we belong.

From Uncle Moshe's fancy house, we move to a small three-room apartment in a two-story building where three other families live. The building is one in a row of identical buildings separated by courtyards with bare soil, other than a few sparse, thirsty, tired trees that are waiting for the winter rain.

A rectangular wooden dining table covered with a tablecloth that Aunt Rachel embroidered herself stands at the center of the living room, the largest room in the apartment. At mealtimes, the embroidered tablecloth is replaced with a plastic tablecloth that can be wiped clean. The couch opens up into a bed when needed, and there's a dresser with a glass case displaying silverware and wine glasses, an ornate wooden clock that looks like an antique, and a few framed family photos around it. It's not fancy but it feels pleasantly homely.

Gadi gives us his room and helps us get organized for our first night in our new home. He'll be sleeping on the living room couch. On particularly hot days, he sleeps on the balcony. He's clearly happy to welcome in the only cousins he has, and even though he's younger than us, he feels responsible for our well-being. He makes us feel welcome, and even Suzy softens and says that he's a nice Jewish boy.

* * * *

Uncle Moshe keeps his promise and accompanies us to church every Sunday. Suzy's fears are alleviated, and her health improves.

In the mornings, Gadi walks with us to our Hebrew class. We've joined a study group for immigrant youth from a variety of countries. We stick out because of our convent uniform and the crucifixes around our necks. Our Hebrew has improved fast and we're top students again, just like we used to be.

On our walk to Hebrew class and back, people stare at us and spit on the sidewalk. I ask Gadi using hand gestures and my poor Hebrew, "Why are these people spitting?"

He points uncomfortably at my crucifix. Gadi explains firmly to anyone who spits or stares at us in wonder and to the neighborhood children who tease him for having Gentile cousins, "They're Jewish, but they believe in Jesus because they grew up in a convent. That's what saved them from Hitler. May his name and memory be erased."

Feeling little by little that I'm on a journey and coming to terms with my Jewish identity, I adopt the way he presents us. I keep saying to myself, I'm a Jew who believes in Jesus, I'm a Jew who believes in Jesus. I try to get through to Suzy and convince her that she should also present herself this way, and I state, "Inside you're a faithful Christian and you have the right not to feel Jewish. I'm sure that God, Jesus, and the Holy Mother understand our situation and are watching over us."

* * * *

In the afternoons I work with Aunt Rachel at the kiosk. It's hard work and the hours are long. Suzy stays at home to clean the apartment and prepare dinner for the family. She goes to a lot of pain in the small, narrow kitchen, which has just a simple table to work on that can only sit two, a low, narrow cabinet with a few drawers on the side that barely open (with an annoying squeak), an ice box to keep the food cool, and a kerosene burner for cooking on. Gadi offers to help her, and at the same time he helps her to improve her Hebrew while laughing and enjoying her mistakes. Once Suzy asks Gadi, "Which egg do you like to eat, a soft bald egg or a hard bald egg?"

It takes him a second to understand her and he answers as he breaks into rolling laughter, "I want a hairy egg." He immediately explains his answer, which only confuses Suzy, and she smiles in good spirit. "You must have meant a soft-boiled egg and a hard-boiled egg."

At dinner, he tells us with a grin how he answered her, and from then on, it becomes a standing family joke. "Today we're having hairy eggs."

We're used to combining work and studying and I'm starting to feel like part of the family. I don't miss the time after I left the convent. I remember those days as gray and without any real connection with the people around me. It felt like there was a wall between us. Sometimes I sin by thinking that maybe I'll have a better future here in Israel than I could have expected there, without family. Is it possible, I ask myself, that the Mother Superior was right, and that I'm here among my people? Suzy, on the other hand, still plans on joining the order of nuns one day. She still has a few more years before she can fulfill this dream.

The summer vacation months are about to end and our lives are going to change with the coming of fall. I feel that every shift in my life is followed by a small change in who I am. I hope the change is for the better.

Chapter 29

Summer vacation is ending in two weeks. We're invited over again to Uncle Moshe's. As we walk in, out of the corner of my eye, I see Uncle Moshe stuffing an envelope into his brother's pocket. A stack of bills peek out. He doesn't seem to be trying very hard to hide what he's doing. Does he want me to notice?

We all wait on the nice terrace. A soft voice inside me whispers to me that this time, too, the get-together is about me and Suzy. I feel tense, expecting another change in our life, with all its upheavals. What does the future hold for us?

Aunt Rachel and Uncle Dov are excited, and this time they're dressed in their finest clothes, perhaps they've overdone it, in contrast to Aunt Hela's noble, cold, and restrained elegance. I prefer Aunt Rachel, but I have respect mixed with hidden envy for Aunt Hela. As usual, Gadi picks freely from the refreshments waiting for us on the sideboard on the side of the terrace.

Against my will, I find myself comparing Gadi's free childhood with my own. Convent life was strict, but Suzy and I were good. We were treated extremely well. Most of the nuns were fair to the children who kept to the strict rules, such as being allowed to use the bathroom only at certain times. But there were also tough, cruel nuns who humiliated and hurt the girls. I remember harsh scenes, punishments of kneeling on salt or corn. Most of all, I'll never forget the five-year-old girl who got up at night to go to the bathroom and drank the water that was intended for our morning bath. She received a beating for these two sins.

I'm still trying to find an explanation for the good way in which Suzy and I were treated. Why were the nuns careful not to hurt us? Why did they try to hide from us those times that they behaved badly? Did they feel the sympathy the Mother Superior had for us, and were they afraid that we'd squeal on them?

My thoughts are interrupted when Uncle Moshe gets up from his chair and smiles at me. As usual, Aunt Hela translates for him, "Dear, sweet Rita, you're all grown up now. It's time for you to choose a profession so that you can earn a living and stand on your own two feet. At this point, your choice is quite limited because of the partial education you received at the convent. Uncle Dov and I have looked at your current options, and we'd like to suggest a couple: You can go to a nursing school that has a boarding residence. It's a three-year course, and you wouldn't be earning a salary, only pocket money. Your other choice is to take a short, three-month course in childcare. You can start studying and living in Beit Hahalutzot, the Pioneer House, here in Tel Aviv. The choice is yours.

"The school year is about to begin and we have to find a school for Suzy. It's not easy. For some time now, I've been looking for a suitable place for her. Being religious, we need to find a religious girls' school for her. There are religious boarding schools for girls in a few places around Israel, and they're in great demand because of all the young Holocaust refugees. Unfortunately, they're refusing to accept Suzy who declares that she believes in Jesus and bears a crucifix. I'm trying to convince the supervisors of the religious boarding schools to be more lenient with her, because she was born Jewish and lived among the Gentiles. I believe in the verse that says: 'Whoever saves a single life, saves the whole world.'

"Unfortunately, after I was unable to find a religious boarding school or a religious school for her that was willing to accept her, I appealed to rabbis of the highest authority to intervene to reverse the decision, but they, too, have refused. The school year starts in a few days and I still don't have a solution for her."

Suzy is huddled next to me. I can see how angry she is; how afraid to say what she wants. I dare to speak for her. "Suzy's place is in one of the excellent mission schools."

Uncle Moshe's face turns alternately pale and red, and he answers me in a firm voice while waving his finger at me, "No, that's not going to happen. I won't let my niece, a daughter of Israel, whom I saved from the Gentiles, study in the mission. Even a secular Jewish school is better than the mission."

No one says a word. Suzy breaks the silence by standing up, and trembling all over, saying in a voice that, despite being weak, cuts through the air, "I don't need saving. Mother Mary and her Son Jesus are the ones who saved me from the clutches of the Nazis and it's in them I place my trust."

Uncle Moshe wipes cold sweat from his face, covers it with his trembling hands, and lowers his head.

And that's how Suzy's future is decided.

* * * *

I toss and turn all night long. My heart goes out to Suzy and I'm afraid of the bad effect it's going to have on her. How will she react? How will she pick up the pieces of her damaged soul when she's up against such a strong force of faith? Her faith is also strong but her ability to defend it is weak. At first it seemed like Uncle Moshe understood us. He even allowed us to go to church. Did he think that with time we'd grow away from our faith? Is the time he gave us over?

Suzy needs the freedom to practice her faith as she pleases. It's the source of her strength, and if her strength is destroyed, she won't last. This is the first time that I've been angry with God. After all, He has the authority, doesn't He? I'm angry at the injustice He created in His kingdom toward children who so believe in Him, and He's not there for them. Where is the Savior who saved her until now? And why is the Messiah of the Jews taking so long?

Frightened by the germ of doubt gnawing at me, I kneel by my bed, cross myself, and pray, "Holy Mary, mother of Jesus Christ, pray for me, a sinner. Restore my complete faith and help Suzy deal with the upheaval that's threatening her. Amen."

The following Sunday, Aunt Rachel is the one who accompanies us to Mass at the church in Jaffa.

While we wait in the courtyard for Suzy to come out of Mass, I surrender to the rays of the late summer sun that's illuminating the valley as it drops down to the sea, the color melding with the clear blue of the sky.

Chapter 30

While we wait for Suzy to come out of church, Aunt Rachel asks me in Hebrew spiced with Yiddish, "Rita, have you decided what you'd like to study?"

"I'm still trying to decide, but I think I'll choose the childcare course."

I say the word "decide" in German and translate it into Hebrew using the pocket dictionary I carry with me in the secondhand purse she gave me recently. I have trouble pronouncing the words and we both laugh in good spirits.

It's hard for me to choose between nursing school and a short childcare course. Clearly, in the long run choosing nursing would be better, but the idea of boarding for another three years doesn't appeal to me. It's not easy for me to admit to myself that I'm sick of any framework that reminds me of the convent. I want to determine my own life and earn my own living right now.

The idea of looking after small children came to me perhaps from my need to atone for burying the suffering of the children at the convent, especially the helpless orphans who were treated badly by the more irritable nuns. This while Suzy and I were treated particularly well. I've kept the difficult memories buried deep inside me, and now I have to prove to myself that those rigid, sometimes cruel methods of education can be corrected.

Aunt Rachel interrupts my thoughts, "It's the holiday season soon. Rosh Hashanah—the Jewish New Year—is already next week, at the beginning of September, and Yom Kippur is soon after, and then Sukkot. Tomorrow we'll go, you, Suzy, and I, to buy you nice clothes for the Holidays, and everyday clothes, because it's time for you to stop wearing the convent uniform. You're not there anymore. During the Holidays, you won't be able to come to church. And after the Holidays, you, Rita, will start studying and move to Beit Hahalutzot."

"And what about Suzy?"

Aunt Rachel lowers her head and answers without looking at me, "You know, Rita, it's complicated with Suzy, she's not prepared to understand her situation. She's digging her heels in by refusing to adapt to her environment. It's not easy to find a school that'll accept her. We'll keep looking."

Her words make me angry. I don't restrain myself and I snap, "It's you who doesn't understand her situation! I think it was Uncle Moshe who told us at the time, when he tempted us to go to Paris with him, that 'one cannot take away a person's experience of faith, they have to want and feel it.' Now he's doing the opposite of what he said. There's no one way to believe in God, so don't force your ways on her, let her be, she's suffering. Right now, her place is at the mission school. Her faith is strong but she's too weak to fight for it, and I'm afraid for her wellbeing."

The oppressive silence is broken when the church bells ring and overwhelm me with memories of the convent. When Suzy comes out of Mass she's sobbing, her shoulders are shaking, and her face is pale. I run over and take her arm.

"What happened?" I ask when I can feel inside that there's no need for her to tell me. I can guess what happened.

"The priest can't help me. No one can save me."

I wipe away her tears, hug her tenderly, and beg her to tell me what the priest said.

"'I can't, he told me. I'm not allowed to. I'll add you to my congregation when the time comes, after you reach adulthood. But now you have to lower your head and wait. Your faith will be there inside you and will protect you.'"

Suzy withdraws and sighs. "I'll be like the Jews were in Spain, just the other way around."

Aunt Rachel jumps up and says, "What do you know about the Spanish Jews and what they went through? It's not the fifteenth century, and no one is forcing you to convert! Or to hide your religion. How can you even compare when you were just in church?"

I intervene, "When we were on the ship, when Uncle Moshe deceived us, Volk spoke against the Christians to convince us that not all faithful Christians are good, and he told us about the Spanish Inquisition against the Jews. Suzy's a very smart girl and she thinks that refusing to allow her to attend the mission school and send her to a secular school is an attempt to force her to hide her religion. This makes her feel like she's being forced to convert."

Sullenly, Aunt Rachel stands up and starts walking home, and we drag along behind her, heavy and sad.

* * * *

A cool fall wind greets us on our way to celebrate Rosh Hashanah at Uncle Moshe's house. I'm wearing my new, fancy, long, white skirt that flares out and a white button-down shirt with long sleeves over it. The new shoes I'm wearing are a bit tight on my toes, after they were free all summer long in the men's sandals we bought back in Paris. Suzy refuses to come, she's still digging her heels in.

The atmosphere on the streets is festive, and a lot of families are walking around, some to synagogue, others directly to their family meal. I'm enjoying being part of the atmosphere, and I'm not nervous, like I am when Suzy's around in these situations, especially as I've hidden my crucifix under my shirt collar. This is my first family holiday in Israel.

The dining room is bright white and the table is softly-lit and set with fancy dishes and shiny silverware on a pale tablecloth. Two silver candlesticks with white candles are standing in the middle of the table. There are sauces with honey alongside slices of apples scattered along the table.

After hearing the blessing, "May the year and its curses end and the year and its blessings begin." I imitate everyone around me, dip slices of apple in honey, and say Amen along with them. Just in time, I stop myself from crossing myself until I can bend over to do it without anyone noticing.

The sips of wine, the wonderful aroma and taste of the food, so familiar from my childhood, help me to relax. I don't sit quite so straight, which was a strict rule at the convent. Pleasantly relaxed, my body slouches and images from the past unfold before my eyes of the only Passover meal I remember having at my grandparents before the persecution and riots began in Berlin. The holidays become interwoven with the holidays I so loved at the convent. Feeling sweetly fuzzy, I think about the fact that we all have the same God, and He's everywhere. He's here together with my family, in this land which from now on is my land. A few more sips of wine put a smile of self-satisfaction on my lips and I say to myself, I benefit from having two worlds, Jesus is still who I lean on, and maybe another messiah will come and I'll win twice.

When the alcohol wears off, I return to my room and persuade Suzy to have a taste of the holiday meal I brought home for her. Pushing away the food when I hold it out to her, she mutters angrily through tight lips, "I won't eat from the hand of the Great Inquisitor."

I muster all my strength and say softly, "The Jews of Spain were saved because they followed their religion in hiding. Adopt their way, I beg you. Keep your faith within you and don't provoke the community around you. The priest said the same. Listen to him. I'm afraid that your strength won't last. The choice is yours."

Chapter 31

I wake up into silence. Only Suzy, who's still asleep, is home with me. My full stomach from yesterday's dinner reminds me that today is Yom Kippur. Our family must be at the synagogue, and we have a day off. It's a special day for us too, the first since we've been in Israel that we're alone. I feel like a bird and that someone's forgotten to lock the gate to my cage.

I shake Suzy to wake her up and say, "Get up, my bird, we have the day off. It's Yom Kippur today and everyone's at the synagogue. I have an idea. Since we've been here, we haven't been to the beach yet, we've only seen it from a distance from the church hill. Today, we can go to the beach on our own without an escort."

Suzy, who of course didn't come to eat the final meal before the fast began yesterday, didn't hear the explanations that I did. She sits down with her eyes half-closed and stammers in a whiny voice, "Why the sea? Again? Where are we going now?" Then she slumps back down on the bed and pulls the summer blanket over her head.

I don't give up. I tell her over and over about my plan while I help her to get dressed. I drag her to the kitchen, force her to eat a few chucks of challah dipped in hot milk, and to drink the rest of the milk. I put a bottle of water in my purse along with two meat sandwiches and leftover slices of apple from last night's meal. I try not to take too much so that no one will notice.

We go outside. What a strange sight we see: There are no cars on the street, only cheerful children racing around on bicycles and scooters.

"Do you know the way to the beach?" Suzy asks.

"No, I'll ask." I stop a boy who almost runs me over with his bike. He stops with a screech and I ask him for directions.

"What are you, tourists?" he asks in bewilderment, then patiently tells us how to get there. I really do feel like a tourist, and my accent also betrays me.

The salty smell of the sea confirms that we're going in the right direction. As we get closer, we see more and more people, young and old, couples with and without children. They're wearing sandals and skimpy clothes that barely cover their tanned bodies. They must also be on their way to the beach. We can see the sea now, getting wider and wider the closer we get until it fills the entire view.

It's a bright day, still summer but the sun's no longer at its peak. We sit down on the dry sand, far from the edge of the waves that make it to the shore. We don't want to get wet. We stare at the sea, almost devouring it with our eyes. It's the same blue as the sky. The air is fresh and we can breathe freely. It's a real day off. Suzy, self-absorbed, stops sifting the sand between her thin, sandy-colored fingers and says in a dreamy tone, "If I knew how to I would swim across the sea back to where I belong."

I go along with Suzy and challenge her with a smile. "Even if you become an excellent swimmer, at some point you'll get tired, and then who will come to help you?"

Suzy answers me playfully, "I'll climb on a whale and steer it to my chosen destination."

"And where exactly is your chosen destination, and who'll be waiting for you there?"

"Representatives of an African missionary monastery along with an African congregation who'll welcome me with dancing and drums."

We both start laughing. "Great, well good luck then. But send the whale back for me, maybe I'll join you sometime." Then I add, "The sea air's having a great effect on you. You're getting your sense of humor back. You lost it for a long time. Let's eat now, I'm thirsty and hungry. You should also eat so that you'll have the strength to go back."

While we're eating, I stare at the tanned bodies of the people on the beach. I envy how liberated they seem, so lacking in shame over their naked bodies, even the girls. I can feel their pleasure from the ease and gaiety with which they enter the water and lie down to dry on the sand when they come out. I'm embarrassed to see couples kissing shamelessly.

"I'm tired," Suzy says and suggests that we go back.

I nod and we pack up.

On the way back she surprises me with a question, "What does Yom Kippur signify?"

"That's precisely what Uncle Moshe explained to me yesterday during dinner. It's the Jews' special day when they ask God to forgive them for the sins they've committed throughout the year. They pray all day in the synagogue and fast to show how repentant they are."

"But the people who were at the beach didn't attend synagogue and pray, and I noticed that they were also eating. Aren't they Jewish?"

"They're Jewish because they were born Jewish, but they're secular like Papa was. He didn't believe in God, but he did ask me to remember that I'm Jewish. It was important to him that I know that I'm part of the Jewish people just like him even if he wasn't religious. I remember that on Yom Kippur Mama used to force him to go to synagogue and she'd send me with him so I could tell her if he really went or not. She'd stay home to look after you because you were a baby."

Suzy thinks a bit about my explanation. "You know Rita," she says eventually with a smile that she tries to hide. "The faithful Jews make life easier for themselves. Once a year, they fast for a day, ask for forgiveness for the entire year's sins, and that's it. We Christians confess our sins every Sunday and the priest gives us penance to do so that He'll forgive us."

I contemplate her statement and reply, "First of all, I don't think Christians have to confess every single Sunday, and I don't know what the Jews pray for when they're in the synagogue. Don't jump to conclusions. We all believe in God and ask for forgiveness for our sins and that's what's important."

"What's wrong with you, Rita? Do you think there's no difference between our faith and that of the Jews?"

I have no desire to get into it again. I'm tired of the arguments about religion and I pick up my pace without answering.

We get back to find Gadi at home, and he's been worrying about us.

"Where have you been? I was scared when I didn't find you here. Where did you go?"

"We went to the beach and it was wonderful. What did you think? That we ran away and wouldn't come back? Even if we wanted to, we couldn't. Why aren't you at synagogue?"

"Yes, you caught some color, but why didn't you leave a note?"

"I thought you'd all come back only in the evening. Why did you come back early?"

"Kids only fast for half a day, will you eat with me?"

Chapter 32

Immediately after Yom Kippur, small hut-like constructions they call sukkahs pop up on terraces and in gardens like mushrooms after the rain. The neighborhood kids happily drag home green palm tree branches to be used as roofing for the sukkahs. Gadi joins the other tenants in the building, who are building a common sukkah downstairs. They stick four poles in the ground and wrap four white sheets around them to make the walls, which move slightly in the wind announcing that fall is on its way.

When I get back from working at the kiosk and the sun is already about to set, I'm surprised to see Suzy fully engrossed in making colorful paper decorations for the sukkah walls, just like she used to make for the Christmas tree.

"I couldn't say no to Gadi. He asked me to help him with the decorations so that we could win the prize for the most beautiful Sukkah in the neighborhood," Suzy says apologetically as she lowers her eyes when she sees the question in my smiling eyes. Gadi, I think to myself, may very well be the kind soul who'll help her out of the darkness she's enveloped herself in.

"Suzy's decorations are wonderful," he declares from the top of the ladder. He hangs the colorful paper chains she made from links of different sizes. They create a surprising pattern. She made paper balls that open and close like fans, and wove together a rainbow of colors to create square or round decorations. Gadi can't stop showering her with compliments. "You can't even buy these in a store. They'll probably win us the first prize."

Unrelated, he quotes his Bible teacher, who claims that "Sukkot is a joyful holiday and people of all nations are welcome to sit in the sukkah because it's a house of prayer for everyone. They are sukkahs of peace."

Suzy consents to Gadi's detailed invitation to join the celebration in the sukkah after she learns carefully that Uncle Moshe won't be there.

I'm filled with hope that Suzy's aching soul will heal. But life has its own plans. A plan that's good news, as Aunt Rachel sees it, but that worries me: They've finally found a school that's willing to accept Suzy. It's a secular agricultural school for girls in Moshav Nahalal. It's far from Tel Aviv, mainly in terms of transportation. The very next day, on Simchat Torah, the last day of Sukkot, Aunt Rachel will take Suzy to Nahalal and I'll move to Beit Hahalutzot to begin my three-month childcare course.

Again, Suzy's face turns gray with fear of the future and I think to myself how many transitions life has given us each to go through. They require so much fortitude. Is Suzy strong enough to survive?

In light of the news that I'm leaving to study and live somewhere new, I debate with myself how I should present myself to my future classmates. Should I declare my faith publicly or would it be better not to stand out and to hide my prominent crucifix? I'm fed up with everyone staring at me, with the looks of bewilderment, anger, and disgust. Some people even spit at me. My belief in God and in Jesus, His representative on Earth, is what gives me strength. Is hiding my crucifix under my clothes wrong? I wonder what the Mother Superior would tell me if I could share my predicament with her. I remember how she calmed me down when I was afraid to play the role of Mother Mary in the Nativity play, knowing that I'm Jewish.

At night, she answers me through a dream, "There's no one way to worship and serve God." How good the calm that envelops me feels when my doubt is removed.

* * * *

Today, on my way home from working at the kiosk, I look for and find a tourist store. I walk past it a few times before I muster up the courage to stop and go in. I choose a thin chain and a small silver-plated cross. My hand trembles as I hand over the little money that I've saved from the pocket money that Aunt Rachel gives me. I'm afraid of telling Suzy that I'm planning to replace my prominent crucifix with a small cross and to hide it under my winter clothes. I'll do it as soon as Suzy moves to Nahalal on the morning I start my course.

On the day before Simchat Torah, Gadi and Suzy help me pack my things and we move them to Beit Hahalutzot so that I don't miss the first day of the course, which begins right after the holiday.

"We're there," Gadi chirps happily and proudly leads us to the entrance connecting two adjacent double-story brick buildings. The buildings are like cubes with straight lines and a row of windows that are also square. They radiate an inviting simplicity. After checking that my name is on her list, a kindly woman leads us to a sparkling clean room. It's very modest with basic furniture and it has three beds.

Gadi peeks out of the room window and says with his characteristic glee, "Rita, you're so lucky! You can see Meir Park from here, and it's very close to us. Let's stop there on our way home for Simchat Torah. It's our last day before we say goodbye."

The woman who welcomed us earlier invites us to have a cold drink in the reception area and explains that the residence building is for older girls without family, mainly new immigrants. They learn Hebrew here, and various subjects such as sewing, cooking, knitting, and weaving. It's all free of charge and we can also take other external courses with external funding. She shows us around and we meet the other residents, who are occupied in a number of ways. They're all girls around my age. For a moment I disconnect and count all the weeks that I've had no friends. Maybe it'll be different here. I like this place.

On the way back we stop at Meir Park. It's quite big and I like that it's wild, not like the formal gardens in Paris. We sit in the shade of the tangled trees, relax after the exciting morning, and watch people on the large lawn with a fountain in the middle.

"It's beautiful here," I say. "I'm happy that I'll get to live so close by. I hope that I'll be able to spend time here in the future."

Out of the corner of my eye, I realize that I'm making Suzy sad and I immediately try to comfort her. I put my arms around her and say, "I'm sure that you'll also have beautiful gardens and make good friends in Nahalal."

We don't spend the Simchat Torah holiday with the family. It's our last day together before we have to separate for a long time. Instead, we pack Suzy's few belongings for the long journey to Nahalal. Gadi helps us pack and his kind attempts to cheer us up are wasted on us.

Suzy takes her time carefully folding her nun uniform, her movements more like a caress. The uniform is already worn thin. Eventually she breaks her silence, "The convent uniforms are my memories. They're my life's journal, and they'll wait for me until I return to them."

When we're finished, Gadi realizes that he has to give us our space and he promises to come and say goodbye to us after the celebration in the synagogue.

Before we go early to bed, I tell Suzy a dream that I make up on the spot, "In my dream last night, the whale that was supposed to sail you across the sea to your chosen destination appeared and said to you, 'I'm old now, I've had enough of long journeys and I won't be able to sail you away. I ask you to have the patience to wait until you can join the convent in your homeland and do the work of your Lord Jesus. That's my suggestion. You'll be able to get to the convent on foot, and if you get tired, I understand the language of the animals, and with my position, I can have a donkey at your disposal to take you to Jerusalem, where you'll find a convent to suit your desires.'"

Smart and sweet Suzy smiles at me for the first time on this sad day and responds, "I love you, Rita, your fabricated dream is wonderful. I'll try to follow the whale's advice, and the donkey and I will pick you up along the way to Jerusalem and we'll continue together."

We push our beds together, kneel beside them, and pray silently. With our arms folded on our chests, we fall asleep but toss and turn, just like during our first nights at the convent, when Suzy would crawl into my bed and at dawn I'd take her back to her own bed so that the nun in charge wouldn't catch us.

Chapter 33

The summer is beginning to retreat and fall is on its way, using up its last remaining dry, hot, desert sandstorms. Despite the heavy heat, I'm filled with joy when I get up in the morning for classes. I'm finding them interesting and they take me out of my narrow world and open up a new world for me. The psychology and sociology classes are fascinating, even surprising, with their ability to cast light on the emotional and social processes with their practical consequences. The constant feelings I used to have at the convent over how children should be taken care of, so different from the nuns' ways, are receiving validation that's based on enlightening studies and formulations.

My courses are combined with the practical work of caring for young homeless children; children whose souls need love, attention, and understanding. Who more than I feels them and knows how much they need the caressing touch of my hands. I painfully recall the convent's strict regime toward children who didn't meet the convent's binding time schedules and received painful and humiliating physical punishments as a result.

Fall in Israel is cool and it reminds me of the summers across the sea. The days are getting shorter, and the sun is quick to set. I return to my room after classes and take a refreshing shower. I go down to the guest lounge to join my roommate and friend, Fanny, for coffee. She's a Holocaust survivor and we've become friends. We share stories about the events of the school or work day. I never ask Fanny directly about her life before she came to the residence, but from time to time we share painful and even funny memories. Perhaps they make the pain easier to bear.

* * * *

This evening when I'm in bed and my eyes close, before I fall asleep for the night, I'm startled awake when I realize that I haven't prayed, and Suzy's face, a reproachful look in her eyes, appears before me. Such a thing would never have happened if Suzy was with me. It's easier for me now that she can't oversee my religious devotion, but I continue to pray in secret, hiding it from my roommates,. And I wear my cross under my clothes. I admit to myself with a tormented conscience that I feel calm without Suzy. I realize that I haven't written to her since we parted, and I haven't received a letter from her either.

I get out of bed and when I'm sure that my roommates are asleep, I kneel in prayer by my bed and ask Mother Mary for forgiveness. Then I sit down to write to Suzy in the dim light of the night lamp.

> Suzy, my dear, how are you? September 27, 1950
> I apologize for not writing sooner. It's been two weeks since we parted. The days are very busy, so please forgive me for not having time to write.
> I really want to hear about your new life. Please describe the place and the surroundings to me. How are you managing in the new place with studies, work, the other girls, and praying?
> I'm really happy with what I'm learning. The courses are very interesting and also involve practical work with young homeless children. I don't want

them to bother me with questions, so I hide my cross under my clothes and pray under my blanket. I have a new friend who I share a room with. She's a Holocaust survivor who lost her entire family. We usually meet up after school and chat over a cup of coffee in the guest lounge until dinner time.
Waiting for your prompt response,
Your loving sister, Rita

* * * *

We don't have classes on Fridays, and in the mornings we clean our living quarters. In the evening we have Kabbalat Shabbat before dinner, a kind of service to welcome the Sabbath. It reminds me of my early childhood and engulfs me in sadness mixed with the pleasant warmth of being part of the community I live with. I feel a kind of continuity, a connection with who I was as a young child and with who I am today.

On Saturdays I have a regular lunch invitation from Uncle Dov and Aunt Rachel.

Today, after we finish our Friday cleaning, I'm called to the guest lounge. Gadi has come to surprise me. He came straight from school and is waiting for me with his school knapsack on his back. He hugs me happily and tells me, "Tomorrow we're having lunch at Uncle Moshe and Aunt Hela, and there's a surprise waiting for you."

All my begging to tell me what the surprise is received with resistance and a broad smile. "If I tell you, then it won't be a surprise. I'll pick you up tomorrow on my way to Uncle Moshe."

At night I toss and turn in bed, my imagination running wild and coming up with a list of surprises that I wish for, desires that have been erased. I immediately dismiss them as impossible because I don't want to be disappointed. Perhaps there's good news about Papa? Perhaps they've found a suitable school for Suzy here in Tel Aviv? Or has Uncle Moshe agreed to Suzy continuing her schooling at the mission? Maybe they'll allow me to complete my own schooling, to finish elementary school and complete my high school education before I start working for a living...

On our way to Uncle Moshe's house, I try to milk some information from Gadi about the surprise that's waiting for me. "Do you have news from Suzy? Has anyone from the family been to visit her? I'll only go myself after I finish the course."

Gadi's eyes are smiling when he looks at me, delighting in the pleasure of having a secret. "You won't get me to tell you, and you'll never guess."

The table is already set and waiting for us to arrive. The food smells wonderful. Suzy's not coming to the family get-together. Uncle Moshe smiles happily and invites us to the table.

Before blessing the food, he stands and addresses me in Hebrew: "Dear, Rita. Today we're celebrating your becoming a citizen of Israel. Under the plate by your side, you'll find confirmation of this. Your years without a country to call your own have ended. It's been a long journey. Since you were a child, you've been a wandering refugee, moving from place to place, not belonging, without a homeland. Today, Israel becomes your country. From now on, you're not dependent on anyone, you're your own master. You and you alone can decide where you head to. Let's raise a glass of wine in your honor."

I'm dumbstruck. I can't move. My hands won't listen to me, I can't get up from the chair, and I can't take the glass of wine that Gadi pours for me. I'm trying to digest the significance of being an Israeli citizen. Is this another change in my identity? Like in a fast-paced movie, images flash through my mind; images of a persecuted and frightened Jewish refugee girl who becomes a dedicated Christian, becomes Jewish again but believes in Jesus, and now after being a refugee without a country, I've become an Israeli citizen. Is this a reason to rejoice, to be proud? Will there be no more upheavals in my life? Politely, I smile at everyone in confusion. They look so happy. I bow my head and the only words I can say is thank you.

"Come on, Rita," Gadi, who's standing next to me, says. "Pick up the envelope already." Impatient, he picks up the plate himself and puts the envelope in my hand.

It bears the emblem of the State of Israel and is addressed to me. I regain my composure, open the envelope, and take out an Israeli identity card in the name of Rita Grossberg.

Chapter 34

As I do every day, on my way back from classes, I stop in the guest lounge and wait for Fanny to join me for coffee. In the corner of the room, there's a metal urn with hot water, jars containing a coffee substitute and powdered milk, and a few trays of dry cookies. There's no one but me there yet. While I'm turning on the urn, a tall, handsome young man enters, his naturally light face slightly tanned. He's wearing a gray jacket and blue work pants.

He looks at me with a pleasant smile and says in Hebrew, with a hint of a foreign accent so light I could have easily missed it, "I hope I'm not disturbing you. I've come here to visit my sister, Hannah. She arrived yesterday. I'll wait for her here."

I nod hello and he extends his hand and introduces himself as Ephraim.

"I'm pleased to meet you." I hold my hand out in response. "My name's Rita and I live here."

I wonder about his good Hebrew. I don't know the word "disturbing." He sounds local but without the snarky roughness I've already encountered. He seems a few years older than me, and I find him intriguing. I'd love to learn more about him but I don't have the courage to start a conversation.

Our silence is interrupted by Fanny, who's accompanied by a girl who runs happily toward him. He stands up and they embrace.

She says in German, "Oh, Ephraim, what a wonderful surprise! I didn't expect you to visit so soon."

Holding hands, they become lost in conversation, chatting away and ignoring our presence until I decide to bring them coffee and cookies. She thanks me and then looks at me again, her eyes widen, and she says in German, "I can't believe it! Aren't you the girl from the convent who was with your sister on the Shalom ship? I was on that ship!"

Her question exposes me and makes me uncomfortable. Reluctantly, I answer with a forced smile and in a low voice, "Yes, it's me."

Hannah continues excitedly, "We all knew that you had no idea that you were on your way to Israel, but we were forbidden from having any contact with you so that you wouldn't find out. You were wearing—"

Ephraim notices how uncomfortable I am with her words and he interrupts her. Speaking in Hebrew, he says, "Really, it's such a small world."

I sigh in relief and watch them both.

He then switches to German, gently addressing his sister with a tinge of reproach, "Hannah, Rita will tell us about herself when it suits her. We all have a life story that only we are allowed to share."

I'm surprised by his sensitivity and words, and a pleasant warmth spreads through my body. I smile with gratitude at him. I feel a thread of closeness stretching between us, at least from my direction.

For a moment no one says a thing. I try to find a way to break the silence. I muster up the courage to speak, a question hidden in my words, "You speak Hebrew so well."

"That's right, it's a long story and right now I have to go. I'll tell you when I come again next week." He hugs his sister and says goodbye.

I watch him as he leaves, and he turns back and smiles as he's leaving. It feels like the smile is for me, but maybe I just think that, and the smile isn't specifically for me.

* * * *

Ephraim visits his sister twice a week on fixed days, and on those days, I go to the lounge earlier. When he arrives, my heart skips a beat and monitor the intensity of the smile he gives me when he sees me.

He keeps his promise and tells us his story. "I was born in 1925, here in Palestine, in Tel Aviv. Our parents are of Polish origin and my father was a Zionist. My mother couldn't find her place here, so in 1933, when I was eight years old and beginning third grade, we returned to Poland. For a long time, I continued to speak Hebrew with my father. That's how I kept it up, although it was the Hebrew of an eight-year-old."

I'm delighted to discover that we share a similar fate, which brings us closer, and unlike my usual self, I interrupt him and say, "I was also eight years old when we fled from the Nazis in Germany, where I was born, to Belgium. I didn't forget my German. Where do you know German from?"

"I'll keep you in suspense until I visit again. Now it's your turn to tell us about yourself."

Moved, I tell my story. "My father moved to Germany from Poland. He was planning to study, but he couldn't because he was a refugee without citizenship. He was a refugee all his life. When the persecution against Jews in Germany became worse, he put me and my little sister, Suzy, onto a train to Belgium. Jewish children were still allowed to travel by train, but he himself stole across the border to Belgium. We met him at the station in Antwerp." I stop, take a few sips of water, and continue, my voice trembling. "My mother stole across the border before us, it was still winter, and on the way she caught pneumonia. I never saw her again, and no one told me that she'd died. To this day I have no details about what happened to her. For ten years Suzy and I expected her to return."

I'm forced to stop here because I'm overwhelmed by tears. The memories are terribly painful and they've been locked away and repressed for so long. Ephraim brings me another glass of water, takes a handkerchief out of his pocket, and wipes my face. I close my eyes and surrender to his care. When I go up to my room, I look at myself in the mirror.

Fanny smiles at me and says, "Since you met Ephraim, you've been very attached to the mirror."

I blush and she adds, "You look fine, you're not a glamorous beauty but you have a sweet and innocent face that confuses and intrigues anyone who sees you, because your eyes are so big and smart."

That night I toss and turn again in my bed, a painful question racing through my head: Could Ephraim be treating me like a father treats his daughter? After all, he's six years older than me and surely there must be more beautiful and attractive girls for him than me?

Chapter 35

This morning, after a sleep-deprived night full of dreams, in which Ephraim's face smiles at me and I yearn for his embrace, and evil scheming nuns interfere in my dream and accuse me of the sin of forbidden bodily sensations. I wake up in a panic. What is happening to me?

I drag myself through classes that day with a long face, but when I get back to the residence, I'm filled with a pleasant feeling that tinged with apprehension: Ephraim will be visiting his sister Hannah today and I'll get to see him.

Fanny notices how eager I am to go down for coffee and says to me, "Rita, try to control your mood. It's obvious that you're attracted to Ephraim because you don't take your eyes off him. Go slow, you're too innocent. You've just left a convent and it seems that it's the first time that you're falling in love with a man. He's melted you and impressed you with his ways and manners, but you're vulnerable. Let's first see how the object of your love feels about you so that you don't find yourself disappointed."

I'm embarrassed. I don't answer her, knowing that I don't have the tools to stifle the feelings that are awakening in me. I look at her helplessly.

Fanny takes my hand and says, "I have a plan. This is what we'll do: We'll take our time today and allow Hannah and her brother to spend a little time without us there. Hannah's a nice girl but she's a chatterbox and very curious. She pointed out to me a while back that you, Rita, have been charmed by her brother. I'm sure that she'll ask him what his friendly way with you means. And she's sure to tell me the impression he gives her."

At their next meeting, Fanny still has no answer.

As usual, Hannah is late. She hands me a letter addressed to me that she picked up when she went to the secretary to report a problem in her room. This is the first letter I've received from Suzy. The letter's in Flemish. I can't wait and I read it that instant. The letter is very short, it's undated, and her handwriting is a little sloppy:

> Rita my dear sister,
> How are you?
> I didn't reply sooner because I didn't want to make you sad. This place isn't suitable for me. I get lost among the noisy group of girls and I have nothing in common with them. I'm very, very lonely and I'd be so happy if you came to visit me. The only good thing is that I'm doing well in my studies but that only makes those shallow girls angry. They say that I'm arrogant and they ostracize me. I don't have anywhere quiet to pray. I'm very weak because I've started vomiting again. I'm drained and I have no appetite, so I'm assigned only light work. I look forward to your visit, and maybe together we'll be able to think of a way for me to leave this place because it makes me very despondent.
> Yours, your loving sister Suzy

I finish reading the letter and a heavy sigh escapes me. I cover my face with both hands. My mouth dries up and I ask Fanny to bring me water. I'm struck with remorse over being too self-involved to try to visit her and to miss a day of school for her.

Everyone asks worriedly what happened and I answer, "It's bad news from my sister. She's at boarding school in Nahalal and I have to visit her immediately. I hope that I'll be able to get a public cab service to her this Saturday. I'll pay for it with the little money I receive for the services I provide in my free time at the daycare center."

After a few moments of silence, Ephraim surprises me with an offer. "I doubt that you'll find a cab service to Nahalal on Saturday. But I'm happy to drive you there on Saturday. I can borrow a van from my employer."

I look questioningly at Fanny and she nods to me to accept the offer.

I ask, "Can Fanny or Hannah come too?"

They both refuse. I'm afraid of being alone with him on such a long journey and I don't know whether to cry for Suzy or to be happy that he's offering to help me.

* * * *

Until I visit Suzy, I find myself feeling angry with that other, new Rita, so different from the old one who took care of her little sister...the strong Rita who for years kept the secret of her Jewish heritage out of the terrible fear that she'd be discovered by the Germans...the Rita who left the convent and supported herself and her sister. Lately I've been a different Rita—soft, bothered by my appearance, and unable to interpret the attention I've been receiving from Ephraim. I try to console myself with how well I've been doing in my courses. They're about to end and then I'll be able to stand on my own two feet.

I decide to go back to being the old Rita.

* * * *

It's a chilly Saturday in the middle of October, and at dawn Ephraim is already waiting for me at the residence door, which is still locked. He's wearing gray trousers and a wool sweater. Under the sweater, he's wearing a brightly-starched white shirt with only the collar peeking out. A sporty flannel jacket completes his appealing look. With a smile, he invites me to join him in the van, opens the door for me, waits until I get in, and goes to the driver's door. The front cabin has three seats and before he starts driving, he hands me a hot cup of coffee and a sandwich, which he takes out of the bag that's between us on the seat.

Surprised, I thank him and say, "You're one of a kind, you think of everything. How did you know that because it's Saturday, the dining room would open later? You really are a good friend."

His gray eyes glimmer in agreement, and we become engrossed in the pleasure of eating, something that brings people closer and makes their time together more enjoyable.

The sky is cloudy and gloomy but the colorful fields of autumn squill we can see through the window makes up for the gloom and lack of conversation in the dull noise of the engine.

Ephraim is the first to break the silence, "Rita, are you willing to tell me about your sister before I meet her?"

"Wow, it's a long story. The Germans occupied Belgium, and my father decided to join the Belgian partisans. That's when he gave me and Suzy to the convent to save us. I was nine years old and Suzy was five. The convent had a school for the peasant children from the area, and for orphans. We worked, studied, and prayed to Jesus and Mother Mary. I knew that I was Jewish, but for my own safety I had to hide it. I believed with all my heart in Mother Mary and Jesus, and I was baptized. Suzy, on the other hand, didn't know she was Jewish. We lived without any real idea of what happened to our parents. It's likely that neither of them survived. We lived in the convent for about nine years. We wanted to become nuns. Suzy was badly traumatized after the war ended, when she found out that she was born Jewish, and I don't think she's recovered from the shock to this day. Our Uncle Moshe tricked us and brought us to Israel against our will. And because he's a rabbi here in Israel, he refused to allow her to attend the mission school, even though she wanted to. The only place that agreed to accept her was the Nahalal Agricultural School, which is secular. Everyone else refused because she openly declares that she believes in Jesus."

My mouth is dry, and I take a deep breath and sip from a bottle of water. Ephraim, who's concentrating on the road, doesn't utter a sound. A wonderful feeling of relief washes over me. I feel so relaxed now that the knot I had locked up inside me has unraveled. There's no need to stand guard and hide anymore. This is me, exposed to Ephraim, whatever his response may be.

Chapter 36

Ephraim's long silence worries me. I squirm inside, wondering if I exposed too much of myself by telling him about Suzy. Did I cross a line? Was I too open with him, and will the truth about me push him away? I stare out the window, seeing and not seeing the passing landscape, and the relief I was just feeling is replaced by pain. I hide the dampness in my eyes from Ephraim.

In the distance, we can see the minaret of a mosque, and as we get closer, he breaks the silence and says, "I need a break. Let's stop to freshen up. There's a cafe in the village and we can walk around a bit. Breathe the fresh cold air before it warms up."

His manners don't change, he opens the door for me, takes my hand to help me get out of the van, and then suddenly and determinedly, he pulls me to him, looks into my eyes and says, "Rita, I think you're afraid that by telling me about Suzy, you've revealed things about yourself as well. Don't worry, I admire your courage and openness. I really like you the way you are, who you are. I really, really like you."

I remain stunned, lower my head, and ask softly, "Only like?"

Ephraim raises my head, smiles slyly but his eyes are kind, and answers with a question, "What more can you ask for, tell me straight from your heart, my dear Rita?"

I become soft all over, I can't believe the words coming out of my mouth in German, words I say in a pleading whisper, "Efraim, I don't want you to like me very much, not even very, very much, I want you to love me."

Startled and embarrassed by the audacity of my words, I try to pull away from him but he suddenly pulls me closer, captures me in his arms, and brings his face close to mine. My lips open of their own accord and surrender to a long, soft kiss that takes my breath away. The wonderful church organ starts playing in my head, and the choir starts singing along.

Ephraim whispers in my ear, "A kiss is better than words."

Am I dreaming? I feel giddy and I collapse limply into his arms with a pleasure that I've never experienced before. We cling tightly to each other, beyond space and time, which are standing still. I don't want this to end. When I tremble with pleasure, Ephraim says while stroking my neck and sliding his hand along it, "Oh, Rita, I long to be close to you and feel your body, but we have to continue our journey, and it's also getting cold." He pulls away from me and, holding my hand, pulls me to the van. Ephraim clears the seat beside him and suggests I lie down next to him with my head on his lap.

After I snap back to reality, I ask him, "Aren't we stopping at the cafe?"

He strokes my head and trying to hide his smile, answers, "Oh! The coffee? It was an excuse to get you out of the van. It's less comfortable, expressing love inside."

I'm left speechless for a few seconds, oscillating between feeling insulted at being poked fun at and his indirect declaration of love.

I reply, "You're more cunning than you appear! I'll have to be careful with you."

I can see him smiling in the mirror, and he blows me a kiss while trying to hide his self-satisfaction at succeeding in his mission.

We continue driving. Ephraim concentrates on the road, and I close my eyes and relive my moments of pleasure until I hear his voice through my fuzzy thoughts, "We've arrived at Nahalal, I need to look for Suzy's school."

The weather is pleasant now and the fall sun blends in with the exuberant teenagers roaming the streets of the village. Their loud voices can be heard far and wide. Ephraim stops them and asks for directions to the agricultural school. They answer in unison and give us directions. We reach our destination, our van the only sound we can hear. It seems like no one's here.

We walk up to the building, and before we walk in, Ephraim stops and says, "Rita, you should visit Suzy without me. She's not expecting you, and my presence may make you both uncomfortable." He hands me a paper bag. "Here, take this—there's fruit and cookies that I baked for her. I'll find somewhere nearby to wait for you."

I enter the building. There's not a living soul in the entrance hall, and at the sound of my echoing footsteps, an older woman comes out to see who's there. She looks at me with suspicion. My guess is that she's the housemother.

"How can I help you? It's Saturday today, and everyone's gone out, some to their family, and others to enjoy themselves in the village."

"I'm looking for Suzy, my sister."

"Oh! It's good that someone's come to visit her! She's very lonely, she's the only one who stays in her room on Saturday, and she hasn't made friends with the boarding school girls."

I feel a sharp pain in my chest upon hearing the housemother's words and I'm overwhelmed with guilt for not coming to see her for so long.

"She's in the last room down the hall on the right. Is she expecting you?"

I don't answer, I just walk toward her room. My legs feel weak. Instead of being happy to be seeing her, I take some time before I knock on the closed door. Eventually, my hand trembling, I force myself to knock on the door. I hear Suzy's feet shuffling and then her familiar voice asking angrily, "Who's there?"

Emotionally, I answer, "Suzy my dear, it's Rita, open the door for me."

A long moment of silence passes before the door opens and Suzy's shadow welcomes me. She falls into my arms and bursts into tears, screaming with unforgettable pain.

Chapter 37

Her soul-penetrating cries turn into sobs until she regains her breath enough for fragmented words to emerge. "Take me away from here," she says eventually. "I'm going insane from loneliness."

I lead her to one of the three beds in the room and sit next to her. I put one arm around her shoulder, which jabs me it's so thin, and I wipe her tear-stained wet face with my other hand. I take a bottle of water out of my bag and hand it to her.

After a few sips, she relaxes, tries to smile, and says, "Rita, my beloved sister, I apologize for the sad reception. It's wonderful that you've come to take me away from here. I don't have much to pack."

I'm surprised and concerned by her words. She's misinterpreted my visit. Is she losing touch with reality? I don't know what to say. I evade responding and pull an apple out of the bag that Ephraim gave me. "I suggest you eat first," I say, and cut the apple in half with the knife he put in the bag.

I bless Ephraim in my heart for thinking of everything. I peel the apple, remove the hard core and the seeds, and give her half. She holds it to her mouth and just wets it with her tongue but doesn't take a bite. I know from past experience how hard she finds it to eat in stressful situations. I take the apple from her and using the knife, I grate it into a puree like my mother used to when I was sick. I use a cookie to spoon it up and hold it to her mouth. She opens her mouth like a baby, manages to swallow a few bits, and stops when the first signs of gagging appear, which she manages to stop.

The housemother knocks lightly on the door. She appears in the doorway with a tray in her hand, which she places on the dresser next to the bed before turning to me and saying, "I've brought you some broth, a soft vegetable cutlet, and some mashed potato. Maybe you can convince her to eat. She's very weak and if she continues like this, we're considering having her hospitalized."

Suzy waves her hand in dismissal and says, "Don't worry, Rita, it'll pass when I get out of here, I've been through this before."

She manages to sip a little soup and eat a little mashed potato. I think she's doing it for me. She falls silent, withdraws, and then suddenly asks, "How did you get here on Saturday when there is no transportation?"

"I came with a friend who borrowed a van from work. Put on your coat, I'll take you to meet him."

"First, help me pack my few things and we'll get out of here."

I wonder if by saying this again she's trying to coerce me into taking her away, since she's always managed to get what she wants from me, or if she really doesn't understand that I can't just kidnap her. I decide to humor her while leaving the room ahead of her. "If necessary we'll pack later."

Left with no choice, she grabs her coat and follows me.

Ephraim walks up to us and introduces himself to her, "I'm Ephraim, I brought Rita to visit you."

The midday sun is warm and we find a pleasant spot to sit. Ephraim breaks the few moments of oppressive silence, "I'm starving, I've been waiting for you to come out and have a meal with me."

He spreads out a few napkins and places containers with a variety of salads, sliced salami, and slices of appetizing black bread. He prepares a choice of sandwiches, sets them on a tray, and offers them to us. Suzy doesn't share the immense pleasure we get from the food. What a shame. Lost in her own world, she's sitting with her head bowed and her face hidden in her hands. I signal to Ephraim not to try to persuade her to eat.

Then she snaps back to reality and asks in such a sad voice that it makes my stomach turn and my appetite dissipate. "This is just a visit, then, it's not a rescue operation?"

The food sticks in my throat and I lose my words. Hers are direct and sting, and possess an accusation that I can't deny.

Suzy breaks the resulting oppressive silence, "Rita, do you remember after the war when you moved to the Netherlands to work, and I wrote and told you how I missed you and that I was suffering with the family I was living with? You sent me money so that I would come to you. I understand that today you have friends who don't leave you room for me."

Only God knows how much her words hurt me. I have no way to take her out of here. I am once again overwhelmed with guilt for not trying hard enough to visit her sooner and for so long.

Ephraim and I exchange glances, and I can see that he can sense my sorrow. Wanting to help, he tries to explain the situation to Suzy, "Things were chaotic after the war. Without papers, you weren't registered anywhere. Only the Mother Superior took responsibility for you, but she didn't have any legal authorization. Today the situation is different. Rita can't break the law and smuggle you out, and she has nowhere you can hide."

A glimmer of rage and offense flashes in Suzy's sunken eyes. She jumps up from her seat, pounds her fist on her chest, and her mouth twists in an attempt to shout, "I'm not staying here! I'll run away, and if Rita doesn't have place for me, I'll hide at the mission and no one will find me because our Lord Jesus will help me."

Surprised by the force of her voice and frightened by the signs of insanity that she's showing, I move closer, hug her, and say softly, "Suzy, you're the most precious person in the world to me. I'm graduating in two weeks, and then I'll be independent and I'll look for a way to get you out of here."

I don't let go until I feel her relax and she starts crying softly with overwhelming helplessness. I feel that it's not the time to speak sense to her, so I try to bring up her declared intention to run away, "Suzy, you're so weak that you won't survive if you run away, what with winter on the way. You need treatment to make you stronger. After talking to the housemother, I understand that if you let them, they'll help you. But above all, don't lose hope because it'll give you the strength to heal. When you get stronger and I start working after I finish my courses, we'll find a way to get you out of here."

Ephraim, who clearly felt guilty for speaking and triggering Suzy, snaps out of it and pours water for us.

Suzy recovers and asks, "How will you get me out?"

"I'll appeal to Uncle Moshe, he's responsible for you according to the law, and I'll tell him that I can provide for us both. After I work for a few months, I'll rent a place for us to live. For now, I can continue living in Beit Hahalutzot. Pray to Mother Mary to forgive me for not visiting you enough. I promise to come again soon. You should return to your room now because we have to get back."

Sobbing but accepting her fate, she says, "Drive carefully." She tries to smile at Ephraim. "Ephraim, you've found a wonderful girlfriend, and it looks like you're wonderful too. Take care of each other."

She returns to her room, her thin and unstable body bent and crying out with sadness and disappointment.

Chapter 38

Ephraim concentrates on driving and doesn't speak. From time to time he glances at me in the mirror with concern. I'm sitting in the corner, curled up and deep in thought. I can't get Suzy's grief-stricken image out of my mind. Her droopy eyes, her shriveled, unstable body, and the severe disappointment our visit caused her won't give me peace. I try to push away the disturbing thought that maybe we were too late and that Suzy's now physically and mentally ill, that there's no cure. I take a deep breath, pour water from the bottle for myself and for Ephraim, and a heavy, sigh escapes me.

"Rita," Ephraim says. "Tell me what you're thinking, share your pain with me—it may help."

Suddenly, memories from the past flash through my head and I whisper, "In the convent, we were taught that it's better for us to suffer in silence and not to bother our friends."

"On the contrary, it worries me that you're imprisoned in your thoughts. Vent your pain, talk about it. Come, lie down on the seat with your head by my side. I'll listen like a priest in confession, but I won't impose any punishments."

A tiny smile appears on my lips. I lie down on the seat and open up, "Maybe I'm overreacting, but sometimes it seems like Suzy's losing her ability to think clearly. Did you also feel that? She's in terrible physical condition. It's not that she doesn't want to eat, it's that she simply can't. She was too young to deal with her identity crisis. She used to say over and over, 'I'm a faithful Christian and suddenly they're telling me that I'm Jewish!' She preferred to deny it and cleanse herself of the body that's of Jewish origin...she spoke about spiritual elevation that requires of the person to ignore the body's needs by eating as little as possible. I'm afraid that her strength won't hold up until I manage to take her out of Nahalal, and I'm not at all sure that I'll be able to."

Ephraim looks at me and our sad eyes meet in silence.

"I hope you don't blame yourself," he says. "You're a wonderful sister. Suzy's problem is that, unlike you, she can't be flexible and bend in the blowing wind; to adapt and accept reality. She's fighting it without having the tools. But she mustn't despair and lose hope."

With one hand on the steering wheel and the other stroking my head, he states, "You know, I've also been in very difficult situations, and now my reality has completely changed for the better. Maybe she also has better times ahead of her."

I find myself wondering about Ephraim's past and I ask him to tell me about himself.

He looks out at an invisible horizon and says, "I was born in Israel in Tel Aviv before the establishment of the state, during the British Mandate. I was eight years old when, under pressure from my mother, we returned to Poland. We had a carpentry shop that supported us well. When I was fourteen, the war broke out, the Germans occupied Poland, and the persecution against the Jews began. The yellow patch...our carpentry shop was confiscated...and we were sent to the ghetto.

"At the end of 1941, on Yom Kippur, they closed the ghetto and the deportations to labor camps began. I was a strong seventeen-year-old, so I worked in different concentration camps doing various jobs. The conditions were harsh, but knowing carpentry turned out to be helpful. Three years later, toward the end of the war, those of us who could still work were crammed onto trains in the middle of the night. In total darkness, we were taken to the Buchenwald concentration camp, and three days later, they moved us to the Dora-Mittelbau camp. It was a terrible place: We worked day and night in the arms industry for a daily ration of a piece of bread and thin soup, which was mostly lukewarm water."

Ephraim stops, takes a deep breath, takes a sip of water, and continues.

"After three months in the Dora camp, I broke down physically and mentally. I became apathetic and I was no longer able to work. My fate was about to be sealed. And then the camp was bombed by the Americans, a commotion broke out, and I ran toward the food storerooms. The Germans fled, the Americans entered, and the Poles took the Polish youth to camps in their own country. I was in a camp for Polish youth in Częstochowa."

Ephraim stops. The painful memories are obviously exhausting him. My heart goes out to him and I caress his cheek and say, "I see that this is hard for you. Tell me more another time."

We drive on, both of us quiet and lost in our own worlds. I doze off until Ephraim's voice wakes me up, "We're close to Tel Aviv. I'll take you back to Beit Hahalutzot. I'm working tomorrow, and you have your courses. We'll meet on the day I visit my sister, Hannah."

The practical, dry tone of his voice disappoints me.

We arrive at dusk to an irritating drizzle. Again, Ephraim helps me out of the car, walks with me to the gate, looks hesitantly at the expression on my face, which leaves no room for guessing what I'm expecting, but he doesn't respond. He just opens the door to the residence for me and walks back to the van. As soon as I enter the reception hall, he surprises me and comes back. He takes me in his arms and we stand there pinned to each other. He whispers in my ear, "I already miss you."

My disappointment is replaced by a warm, wonderful feeling that spreads through my body and fills me. I hug him back tightly and we stand like that, pinned to each other, ignoring everyone around us, barely able to pull ourselves apart. Giddy and weak in the legs, I go upstairs and shut myself in the shower to relax away from my roommates' eyes.

Exhausted from the intense and tiring day, the mixture of deep sadness, distress, and concern for Suzy's condition, and incredibly sweet moments of pleasure, warmth, softness, and expectation that came true. I don't bother with dinner. Instead, I go back to my room and avoid meeting the other girls, who haven't returned to their rooms yet. I go to bed early, and under the covers, before I go to sleep, I pray to Mother Mary and ask her to heal Suzy and for Ephraim not to stop loving me if he finds out that I wear a cross around my neck. I decide that the next time we meet, I'll remove the cross from its chain and put it back on afterward. Then I ask Mother Mary to show understanding and to continue to protect me.

Chapter 39

After a heavy night's sleep, I wake up very early and bathed in sweat. My body feels too heavy for me. I have a fever, and it's hard to sit up and get out of bed. I go back to sleep. Disoriented by the fever, yesterday's events unfold before my eyes, whirling around with images from our trip to Paris, the church choir singing, the organ playing, the figures of the Mother Superior and Uncle Moshe, and Suzy with her gagging spasms. I see Papa's figure walking away from the train, which is billowing smoke, and I run after him, losing the cardboard doll and her clothes that I loved so much. I find myself in the clutches of fear because I'm hiding the big crucifix from Ephraim's inquisitive eyes.

I wake up in a panic to the dim light of a rainy winter afternoon. A few minutes pass before I regain my composure and find by my bed a thermos of hot tea, two aspirin tablets, a cream cheese sandwich, and a note from Fanny:

> Good morning, Rita. You didn't wake up your normal self this morning. You were burning up. Don't put on a brave face, just stay in bed, drink a lot, and take the tablets to bring your temperature down. The housemother will check on you from time to time to see how you're feeling. See you when I get back, Fanny.

After missing two days of studying and staying in my room, my temperature drops. The memory of our first, delightful kiss rises to the surface of my mind, and I find myself waiting in anticipation to see Ephraim in the afternoon when he comes to visit his sister...and perhaps me too?

The longing I feel comes with doubts and misgivings that perhaps I revealed too much about my feelings and physical attraction to him. Could I be losing control, could the overwhelming physical urges be melting and weakening me? Should I distance myself a little? I hope he'll tell me more about his life story, which he didn't finish. I'm curious and I'd like to get to know him better through his story. I don't want to betray the fact that I can't stop looking into his veiled eyes or to reveal the depth of my feelings, so I come up with a brilliant idea to bring with the puzzle of Notre Dame that Volk gave me on the ship when we next meet. That way we'll all concentrate on the relaxing puzzle while we listen to the rest of his story.

I feel my cheeks flushing when I see him. I look into his eyes... they're smiling at me, and I nod my head hello, scurry off to get cookies and make coffee, and announce solemnly, "Finally, the three months of training to become a certified child caregiver are over. The next time we meet, I'll give you a detailed invitation to the certification ceremony. For now, the important detail is that it's in the morning of the first Tuesday in December. I hope you'll be able to take the time off from work."

"We'll be there, of course we will," Fanny says.

Ephraim nods and adds in a thunderous voice, "Well done to our Rita!"

I whisper in Fanny's ear, "Ask Ephraim to finish his story." I dramatically take the boxed-up puzzle out of my bag, empty the pieces onto the table next to ours, push the two together. "I like jigsaw puzzles. Let's put together this beautiful picture of Notre Dame today."

"What a wonderful idea for an annoying winter evening," Hannah says enthusiastically. "They say this is the worst winter in fifty years, and there's a chance of snow. Let's start with the edges."

Fanny quickly responds, "Wait, before we start the puzzle, Ephraim has a story that he already started telling us. Will you continue? We're all curious to hear how you survived."

Hannah intervenes and turns to Ephraim, "Efraim, I told the girls that you spent time in a few concentration camps until you were sent to the Buchenwald camp."

Ephraim continues his story. We listen while putting the jigsaw pieces together.

Fanny interrupts him when he gets to the part about hiding in the storerooms after the Americans bombed Dora camp just in time to save him. "Devouring too much after being starved can kill you," she says. "Many people died that way."

Ephraim is breathing heavily now. "That's very true," he whispers. "But I was so weak that I only ate the little I was given. Perhaps that's why I survived. In any case, the Germans fled, the Americans entered, and the Poles transferred me as a Polish citizen to a Polish youth camp in Częstochowa."

This is where the rest of his story, which I haven't heard yet, begins. I stop working on the puzzle and focus solely on his words. I don't take my eyes off him, which I don't realize are revealing just how deeply my heart goes out to him.

Ephraim continues his story. "There were Jewish organizations looking for survivors, and they found me, and so, in 1946, when I was twenty-two years old, I arrived in Palestine as part of a Youth-Aliya group."

Excitedly, I blurt out, "My sister and I were found by my uncle, a rabbi from Israel, but we didn't want to leave the convent and come to Palestine. He tricked us."

Ephraim smiles at me and says, "I understand that you went

through a difficult crisis, but I'm glad that fate brought us together."

I smile at Ephraim as my cheeks turn slightly red.

And he immediately continues. "After a few months on a kibbutz, I joined the Palmach and fought during the War of Independence in the Battle for Jerusalem."

Here Ephraim explains with undisguised pride what the Palmach battalions were and how important and difficult it was to break the siege on Jerusalem. He finishes his story, takes a sip of the coffee I made for him. The coffee's cold now and I rush off again to make him a fresh cup.

Fanny, still engrossed in assembling the puzzle, demands to know more, "And after that? It's been over a year since the end of Israel's War of Independence. What have you been doing since then?"

"I work in carpentry, I rent an apartment with three friends, and four days a week after work, I study bookkeeping. Maybe in the future I'll be able to complete high school, which the Nazis prevented me from doing. Then I'll be able to attend university."

Hearing about his ambitions, I feel as proud of him as if he were already mine.

"I'd also love to complete my poor education from the convent school, but my uncles think otherwise. They never asked me, and without means of my own, I have to start working for a living. I've always been a good student and it bothers me that I haven't been allowed to complete my education."

My moist eyes reveal my pain. Ephraim moves to sit next to me and hugs me right there under Hannah and Fanny's watchful eyes.

"Don't be sad, Rita," he comforts me. "Believe that one day you'll make your dream come true."

Surprised by the hug he's giving me in front of everyone, I feel a little dizzy, and I hide my burning face with my hands until

Ephraim lets go, returns to his seat, and says, "Rita, I heard that you've been a little sick, so I suggest we say goodbye early today. Kudos to you for taking the initiative and bringing the puzzle, it's perfect for days like these. Let's put it aside for now and continue working on it when we meet again, as usual, later in the week. And of course I'll come to your end-of-course ceremony."

I go to bed happy and serene, but when I wake up in the morning I feel guilty because I forgot to pray before I went to sleep and I left my cross in its hiding place. Most of all, I feel the weight of hiding my faith and my cross from Ephraim. I can't find the courage to tell him because I'm afraid of losing him.

Chapter 40

The small hall, where the ceremony celebrating the end of the childcare course will be held this morning, has been decorated with small Israeli flags hanging diagonally along the walls. There are big Israeli flags standing on the two sides of the stage with chairs between them for the teachers and the course director, who'll be handing out the certificates. Shivering from the intense cold of December, we're waiting at the entrance for a signal to enter the hall after all the guests are seated. We're all wearing white blouses and long skirts or blue pants. We enter in two rows from both sides of the hall and sit in the front row, which has been reserved for us. Our names are written on the chairs in the same order that we entered in. Mine is right in the middle of the row.

On my way to the front of the hall, I look at the guests and notice Ephraim, Fanny, Hannah, Bella (my other roommate), and Aunt Rachel with Gadi, who's waving to me. I nod at him and smile back. Uncle Moshe and Aunt Hela are out of the country, and Uncle Dov is still at work at the kiosk. After some consideration and after consulting with Ephraim, I decided that it was better not to invite Suzy, not only because of the difficulty involved in getting her here. This, despite the pain in my heart and the guilt I feel.

The atmosphere is festive, and I'm excited. I like being part of a community and feeling the warmth of belonging. While we're waiting for the teachers to go on stage, the image of my communion ceremony in the church, with Papa present, appears in my mind. How I wish Papa was here by my side. He would surely have been happy to meet Ephraim.

The teachers walk onto the stage. The course director says a few words of congratulation to the graduates and calls us one at a time by name to come up to the stage to receive our completion certificate from him. We're called up in the same order that we're sitting, alternately from the right and then from the left. The girls before me take their certificate in their left hand, and shake the teacher's hand with their right. I'm nervous because according to the order, I'm going to be last onto the stage.

Finally, I hear the course director announce solemnly, "And now, our outstanding student Rita Grossberg is invited to come on stage. Rita excelled in the study material, in the practical work in the field with her warm and loving approach to the children she took care of, and in creating a friendly and supportive system with the other students of the department."

A roar of applause rises from the audience. Overwhelmed, I walk onto the stage with a grateful smile on my face.

After we sing the national anthem Hatikvah, the guests are invited to the buffet where there are tiny glasses of red wine and cakes that the girls from the cooking and baking course made. I find myself surrounded by expressions of admiration and affection from my guests and classmates.

Ephraim takes my arm and says, "Well done, our smart and good Rita. Now, we'd like you to introduce us to your aunt."

"This is my Aunt Rachel and my cousin, Gadi, and these are my friends from the residence and my roommates, Fanny, Hannah, and Bella." I hesitate for a second and introduce Ephraim as Hannah's brother.

Ephraim adds with a smile, "In addition to being Hannah's brother, I'm also the friend who drove Rita to visit her sister Suzy on Saturday."

"How is she, and why didn't she come to the ceremony? Aunt Rachel asks.

Gadi asks loudly, "Ephraim, do you have a car? Next time I want to come with you to visit!"

"She's very lonely, she's not adjusting. She wants us to take her away from there," I answer Aunt Rachel. "She's unable to eat again, she's very weak, and she needs medical attention. I'm also worried about her mental state. Now that I've finished my studies, I'll go visit her again before I start working."

Aunt Rachel lowers her head in awkwardness, and says, "I'm sorry to hear that. There was no other solution."

Before the guests disperse, Aunt Rachel pulls me aside and asks me, "Is this friend of yours Ephraim Jewish?"

I'm annoyed by the question, and moreover, I'm not comfortable with the fact that Aunt Rachel realizes that Ephraim is more to me than just Hannah's brother. Defiantly, I reply, "Jewish! Jewish! He was born Jewish! He's a secular Jew like my father, and a better Jew than me."

Aunt Rachel ignores my angry tone. "He makes a good impression." She motions to him to join us and says, "I'd like to invite you both for lunch next Saturday."

Surprised, Ephraim looks questioningly at me and responds, "If it's fine with Rita, I'll gladly come."

After I say goodbye to the guests, I weigh what to do and tell myself that for the first time ever, I have a real sense of freedom. It's the first day after the course ended. I haven't been assigned a job yet, and for the first time in my life I can decide for myself what I want to do. It feels good to be free, but it comes with a shadow of concern because from now on I'm responsible for making my own decisions.

Ephraim interrupts my thoughts and says, "Rita, I took the whole day off to celebrate with you. Since we visited Suzy, we've only met with our friends present. I miss being close to you."

I tremble when he takes my hand, pulls me to him, and whispers as he touches my face as light as a feather, "I'm dying of two kinds of hunger. Can I invite you to celebrate with me? We'll have lunch in a restaurant, and then a movie. What do you think?"

The cold December evening air hits my hot face as we leave the movie. We burst into liberating laughter when we both realize that the only thing we remember about the movie is the heroine's name, Rita. We couldn't tear ourselves apart to watch it. Our bodies were on fire with longing and passion that had been waiting until we could meet in order to break free. The touch of Ephraim's warm hands caressing my body, which gradually relaxes. The only thing stopping me was an internal order from the convent's limits.

In the evening, when I'm alone in the bathroom and still drenched with the physical longing that's shaking me, I put on the cross and feeling sinful as I caress my brazen breasts. This evening they felt the touch of Ephraim's hands for the first time, and my own hands didn't push his away.

I kneel in front of the window and appeal to God, "Why did you make physical contact feel so good when we've been taught for all those years to abstain and view it as a sin."

It's so hard for me to escape the taboo in my education. The prohibitions against the need to love exhaust me, and my love for Ephraim is a source of both happiness and suffering.

Chapter 41

Saturday arrives, and it's very cold. Ephraim and I are having lunch at Uncle Dov and Aunt Rachel. Aunt Rachel has clearly worked hard on the cholent stew that Jews eat on winter Sabbath days. Dov and Gadi are wearing yarmulkes and they've set out a yarmulke for Ephraim next to his plate. He puts it on and says the blessing on the food as if it's something he does every day.

"The cholent is very tasty," he says. "It's the first time since the war that I feel like I'm in my parents' home."

After eating the plums and waiting for the semolina delicacy, Uncle Dov asks Ephraim about his family and about what happened to them, how old he is, how he makes a living, and other questions that to me, seem too nosy.

Ephraim is happy to oblige, even though he's being cross-examined like a potential candidate for marriage. I feel tense and I don't say a word. I'm a little embarrassed by all their questions

Aunt Rachel intervenes, "Come on, Dov, don't you think you're asking too many personal questions?! Ephraim is being patient and polite in answering you, but you're embarrassing Rita."

Uncle Dov immediately shifts uncomfortably in his seat and apologizes, "Oh, sorry, Ephraim, if I'm being too nosy. I heard from Rachel and Gadi that you excelled in your studies. Well done, it's a shame that Uncle Moshe and Aunt Hela couldn't make it to the ceremony."

I ask, "What country is Uncle Moshe visiting now, and what's the purpose of his trip?"

"He's in the United States raising funds for the rescue and absorption of European Jewish children who survived the Holocaust so that they can be brought to Israel. He's there on behalf of the Youth-Aliya organization. They're coming back to Israel tomorrow."

Gadi adds, "It's the same funds that he used to bring you and Suzy to Israel."

It seems to me that Gadi's parents don't like his statement. They change the subject and ask me about my plans.

"I'm on vacation next week," I tell them. "I've had plenty of offers and as a prize for excelling, I've been given the opportunity to choose where I want to work. I've chosen to work in a children's home close to our residence. That way, I can continue boarding at the residence for a few more months for a low price until I can rent my own place, and then I'm planning to bring Suzy to me and arrange for her to attend night school. I hope that Uncle Moshe will be flexible and agree to this."

Before we say goodbye, Aunt Rachel calls me to the kitchen, gives me a bag with packed portions from the lunch we just ate, and says, "Your young man is charming, a little older than you, and you're very young. I hope you know how to take care of yourself and not get up to any nonsense. Guard your boundaries."

I blush, and say, "Don't worry, I was very well educated at the convent."

Gadi asks to accompany us all the way to the end of the street, despite the dry, bone-chilling cold and strong whistling wind. Gadi clearly wants to spend more time with Ephraim and to adopt him as his big brother. I remember what Gadi said about the work Uncle Moshe was doing overseas, and it bothers me but I don't understand why. I feel heavy after the delicious but stodgy lunch, and it's hard for me to walk against the wind.

I ask Ephraim where we're going at this gray time, with cloudy skies promising rain, and I hear myself answering myself out loud, "To be honest, the only place we can both go at this time on a Saturday afternoon is the residence lounge. It's still too early even for the cinema."

Gadi looks at me and asks, "What's in the bag that my mother gave you?"

Before I answer, it dawns on me that the bag of food was just an excuse for Aunt Rachel to take me aside to warn me not to get carried away. I answer Gadi, "Portions of the wonderful food left over from the meal. I turn to Ephraim. "What do you think, Ephraim? Should we take the food to my friends at the residence, or to your friends?"

"I know that Hannah really liked Cholent, so let's go to your residence and finish the puzzle."

Gadi goes home and Ephraim, being a gentleman, takes the bag from me. I take his willing warm hand and say, "Did you notice that they didn't ask how Suzy is? They didn't even mention her. I find it very disappointing. I guess that to them she's a failure and doesn't even exist anymore."

"It's really sad, and you don't know how true your words are," Ephraim replies. "For religious Jews, anyone who leaves the religion or marries a gentile is mourned as if they died. They cut off all ties with the person. Religion can be very cruel, and not just the Jewish religion."

I don't want to be dragged into an argument, but I think to myself that Christianity's not like that. Jesus is merciful and kind, He doesn't take revenge. On the contrary, he turns the other cheek to the enemy who strikes him. Instead of sharing my thoughts with Ephraim I say, "I have to visit Suzy in the next few days before I start work. I think that it would be best to go already this week. I'll take the bus, so I'll have to leave early in the morning to make it back on the same day."

Ephraim pulls me closer, looks at me at length with love and admiration in his eyes, and says, "You're taking on a difficult task with the terrible road conditions these days, even more now because this winter is so bad. I'm happy to come with you. I'll take a day off, I've accumulated vacation days, and this season's weak, so it's a good time to take a day. If you agree, of course."

Tremoring with the surge of attraction I feel for him, I nod my head in agreement, afraid to reveal my overwhelming desire to be with him as I recall the pleasure we shared on our way to Nahalal. I'm looking forward to being alone with him, and at the same time I'm afraid that I'll lose control. I wonder if Ephraim feels the same. Does he also lie in bed at night and relive the memory of our first dizzying kiss? Does he wonder if we'll have another, similar experience on our next trip? He seems to be in better control of his emotions than I am...after all, I'm the one who had a fever after Nahalal, who's whole body ached, and let me not forget that he's a few years older than me....

"A penny for your thoughts?" Ephraim asks with a curious smile.

I try to come up with an appropriate response. "I'm thinking about Suzy, I'm afraid of seeing her." I add a decisive statement to hide what I'm feeling, "Thursday would be best."

"I'll take the day off. This coming Thursday suits me too. We'll leave early and take the bus. Dress warmly. I'll take care of everything else."

We meet up with Fanny and Hannah in the guest lounge, warm up with the coffee I make for me and Efraim, and put the last pieces of the puzzle together to complete it.

Chapter 42

I open my eyes to a gray and gloomy morning. My blanket's fallen to the floor, and I pick it up, pull it over my nose, and listen to the rain bashing on the windowpane. My roommates have already left for work or classes, while I am still off and can get up late. Lying in my warm bed and I smile to myself as I think about seeing Ephraim and my friends in the afternoon for coffee.

A warm feeling spreads through my body in anticipation of tomorrow's trip to Suzy with Ephraim by my side, but very quickly the pleasant warm feeling is replaced with a feeling of distress. I'm afraid to see Suzy and I'm concerned about her future. I wonder if our visit will do her good. It may exasperate her misery and disappointment from the physical world as a whole, which is turning its back on her. I reproach myself, her beloved sister, for being swept up in my blossoming love while she's sinking into loneliness and sickness.

Tormented by feelings of guilt, I suddenly jump out of bed in a panic, kneel by the window, and with the cross still around my neck from last night, I pray silently and fervently for my sister: Holy Mother Mary, please bring relief and calm to my sister, Suzy, who is filled with love for God and His son Jesus. Show me the right way to help her and forgive me if I sin against her when I choose for myself a life of work and love.

I finish praying and stand up. I decide that until I meet my friends and Ephraim in the guest lounge, I'll ease my conscience and volunteer to help in the dining room; like a penance of kind that I inflict on myself. I don't forget to take the cross off. It's still a secret that I'm hiding from Ephraim and my friends. Faith is a support for me, and to that I can now add the emotional and physical closeness that I feel for Ephraim and that I cannot deny or give up.

I head down to the guest lounge and wait for Fanny and Hannah. I can't wait to see Ephraim, and I become uneasy because he's unusually late this time. I breathe a sigh of relief when he walks in with a dripping umbrella. His shoes and the hem of his pants are drenched. I suggest to him to take his shoes and socks off so that we can dry them by the hot kitchen stoves. I tell him to hold up the hem of his pants and ask Hannah to pour him hot tea to warm him up. I go up to my room to grab dry socks and a towel for him. He clasps the hot cup with his long, frozen fingers, which, despite the manual work he does, to my loving eyes they still look refined. These are the fingers that stir my body.

Ephraim turns to me, and I hear hesitation in his voice, "The weather forecast for tomorrow is also bad. What do you think, Rita, should we postpone the trip until the weather improves?"

Feeling a restless urgency to carry out my mission, I answer, "I'm starting work next week, and every extra day that Suzy suffers from loneliness doesn't contribute to her health. Bad weather won't deter me."

A smile of admiration spreads across his face, he salutes playfully, and says, "If it's okay, Commander, I'm with you, Rita. You're an amazon. I'll report here early tomorrow morning and bring two umbrellas and food for the road."

He stays longer today while he waits until his clothes and shoes, which I stuffed earlier with older newspaper to absorb the moisture, are dry. This is what we used to do at the convent, after picking the asparagus in the puddles of melting snow at the beginning of spring."

Ephraim puts on his shoes and is about to leave when the housemother appears suddenly and hands me a telegram.

With a hint of concern, she says, "The telegram was sent from Nahalal to Rabbi Moshe Grossberg, but it's addressed to you. According to the information on it, it was sent this morning, but the bad weather must have delayed it and we only just received it."

Something at the edge of my stomach tightens, sounding an alarm in me. Is it what I feared? I can hear my heart racing and my hands are trembling too much to open the telegram. Ephraim comes to my aid, asks if he can open it for me, and then hands it to me:

> **It is with great sadness that we announce that today at dawn the student Suzy Grossberg was found lifeless. She died in her sleep. Please contact us. Nahalal Agricultural School.**

I remain planted in my chair, my eyes fixed on a point in the distance, and as I crush the telegram in my hand, I say quietly in a broken voice, "God didn't answer my prayers. Suzy died last night in her sleep. Her death hasn't come as a surprise to me. It was her choice. Her death was better than her life, which was full of suffering."

I get up from my chair and head to my room, I need to be on my own. As I walk away, I hear Ephraim say, "Only the righteous die in their sleep."

I lie on my bed and protest to God:

> God! Is death in your sleep the help that You chose for Suzy? Is that all You could do for your righteous follower? Why didn't Jesus see Suzy's incessant pain and suffering? I believed that You were my support, my comfort in times of trouble, where were You?

For the first time since I received the news, I burst into tears over the death of my little sister, and over the comfort I no longer find in my faith.

I won't leave my room until the day of the funeral, which will take place at the Jewish cemetery the day after tomorrow on Friday morning. She'll be buried by her grandfather's side, whom she never knew; the grandfather who is the father of our uncles, Moshe and Dov, and of our father.

Suzy would probably have chosen a Christian funeral and burial, but no one asks my opinion. Uncle Moshe makes the arrangements, and as far as he's concerned, anyone who was born a Jew is to be buried as a Jew.

Chapter 43

A canopy of dripping black umbrellas are huddled together and touching at the Jewish cemetery in Tel Aviv, trying to protect us all from the heavy rain.

Other than our relatives, who came to accompany Suzy on her last journey, three of my friends, Ephraim, and members of the Chevra Kadisha, the society of Orthodox men who perform Jewish burials, are there to make up a minyan of ten men, as required for a Jewish Orthodox burial. I try not to cry but when her tiny body, shrouded in white and looking like that of a little girl, slides into the grave, I break down in heavy sobs followed by everyone around me. The tears merge with the downpour from the sky, which is crying with us.

I wonder if Uncle Moshe's tears are purely for Suzy, or perhaps also for his failure in bringing her closer to Judaism. After all, according to him, that's what's delaying the redemption of the entire nation of Israel. Or maybe he's crying because his conscience is bothering him over his own part in Suzy's harsh fate. In pain and angry at him, I find myself hoping that the last option is true—that not only my conscience is tormenting me for not being there to support her during her difficult times.

Uncle Moshe is breathing heavily, and his voice breaks every now and then and is swallowed up by the whistling wind as he recites the mourners' Kaddish prayer:

Yitgadal v'yitkadash sh'mei raba
b'alma di-v'ra...v'yamlich malchutei

v'yitzmach porkanei v'yikarev m'shichei...
Oseh shalom bimromav, hu ya'aseh shalom aleinu
v'al kol-yisrael, v'imru amen.

As most of it is in Aramaic, Ephraim printed the text for me in Hebrew. From the little I understand, it seems to me that the Kaddish prayer doesn't mention the dead at all, only the greatness of God and His request to speed up the coming of the Messiah and peace:

Exalted and hallowed be His great name
Throughout the world which He has created according to His Will.
May He establish His kingship,
bring forth His redemption and hasten the coming of His Messiah...
He Who makes peace in His heavens, may He make peace for us and for all Israel; and say, Amen.

I ask myself when and who will eulogize Suzy.

I look questioningly at Ephraim, who reads my thoughts and takes it upon himself. "Suzy grew up in a convent as a devout Christian from the age of five to the age of fourteen. To her surprise, she then learned that she was born Jewish. She wasn't old enough to overcome such a significant identity crisis, and what's more, all she wanted was to become a nun. Her sudden removal from her natural environment destroyed her tender soul and her health, and led to her death."

Ephraim is clearly feeling very emotional, and ends by saying, "Suzy is another one of the six million victims of Nazi evil. She was a person who experienced religion very deeply, and her place is in heaven."

I'm not sure that Uncle Moshe feels comfortable with the eulogy, but it's certainly pleasing to Suzy's soul on its way to become one with her God.

Initially, everyone was invited to Uncle Moshe's house for the shiva, but at my request, it was moved to Uncle Dov's home. I explained to Aunt Rachel that Suzy never forgave Uncle Moshe, and her memory should be respected.

On our return from the funeral to sit shiva at Uncle Dov's home until the Sabbath begins, I say to Ephraim what I don't dare to say out loud to my family, "Suzy's not only another one of the six million victims of the Nazis, but also a victim of the power struggle between two faiths—her own, and Uncle Moshe's, and neither is better than the other. They both pray to the same God who belongs to us all. I'll take part in the Jewish ceremonies in Suzy's memory because she was deprived of having the ceremony in the church, the beauty of which overshadows the Jewish ceremony."

Ephraim nods thoughtfully. "I don't believe in God, but everyone should live according to their own faith. You have a point, and I respect the way you're choosing to incorporate your own feelings with the reality around you. You're in my heart, and you're practical and smart." Then he takes my hands and looks straight into my eyes, and says softly, "Rita! I love you so much."

This is the first time he's said out loud what I've been dying to hear for such a long time. I'm still crying for Suzy but at the same time waves of pleasure flood me and rise in my chest. I stroke his beautiful face and say, "It took you quite some time to say those words, which makes them sound so sweet and true. I don't need to tell you how much I love you. It happened the moment I saw you, and in all my innocence I didn't try and couldn't hide it. Sometimes I wonder what someone like you could see in me."

Ephraim pulls me into his arms, silently conveying that I have nothing to worry about. Saying, "I'm yours."

The rain is getting stronger, forcing us to walk faster, and we continue in silence. I cling to him, to his arm around me, supporting me while making me feel dizzy and weak in my limbs and instilling confidence in me that I have someone I can rely on.

We arrive at Uncle Dov's. My relatives are already there and I try to avoid Aunt Rachel's inquisitive glances, which are scrutinizing the blossoming femininity reflected in my flushed face. I make hot tea for Efraim and myself, and in the process I tell them that I'm starting to work at a children's home near the residence and that I'll be coming to the shiva only after work.

During the shiva, I'm horrified when I remember that Christmas is in a few days, and it'll be the first time since I was sent to the convent that I won't be able to attend Mass. It's not the time to ask Uncle Moshe to allow me to attend church, and there's no one to accompany me. I sink into wonderful memories of Christmas rituals. I miss the echo of the wonderful music, the sound of the organ, and the choir's singing that filled the church; comforting sounds that connect us with God and bring us beauty and a taste for life.

The irony of fate is that it's Suzy's death that distances me from faith. I wasn't surprised by the doubts I have regarding religion with all the anger that's built up in me against my God for leading Suzy on a painful path to her death, which drove those doubts. Yet despite my anger, I continue to pray to Mother Mary before I go to sleep with the cross around my neck. I still remove it when I get up at dawn.

After the shiva ends, I go with the family to the grave to recite the prayer, El, Malei Rachamim…God, full of compassion…. It's a prayer for the ascension of Suzy's soul to rest in heaven. I listen to the words.

O God, full of compassion, Who dwells on high, grant true rest upon the wings of the Shechinah (Divine Presence), in the exalted spheres of the holy and pure, who shine as the resplendence of the firmament, to the soul of Suzy, who has gone to her world.

Chapter 44

Suzy's death came as no surprise to me. I had a feeling of impending disaster a long time before her death. But that doesn't prevent me from feeling deep pain and guilt, which sink and burrow into my soul. Suzy's drooping, lifeless face and her dull eyes appear in my painful and disturbing dreams. Only returning immediately to work alleviates my addiction to grief and guilt.

Ephraim is the only person I can share the guilt and anger I feel at myself for not being by Suzy's side during her difficult time. He listens carefully and says reassuringly, "Rita, you were a devoted sister. You mustn't blame yourself. Sometimes we have no control over what happens to us, but we can choose how we react to what happens to us. It was Suzy's choice not to bend to reality and not to keep her faith in a different way without harming herself. She didn't die because of you, and your life is the best way to keep her memory alive."

Ephraim's comforting words are a healing balm that soothes me and helps to dull the pain of her death. He manages to comfort me and I think, What a charming Ephraim I've found.

I wholeheartedly devote myself to my work with the boarding school children I'm in charge of; children who were sick when they were taken out of tents that were being flooded by incessant rain in this cold January. The tents are serving as a temporary housing solution for the influx of immigrants who arrived in Israel en masse immediately after the end of the War of Independence. Most of the children are immigrants and it's hard for their parents to visit them, as they're far away living in tents in transit camps and have no transportation or funds and they don't even speak the language. The country has taken it upon itself to take care of them. The children's age ranges from a few months to six years old. I'm delighted by their every smile when I caress them or hold them. I have a lot on my hands—feeding, bathing, giving medication, cleaning, taking temperatures, performing all kinds of treatments, and night shifts too. The work is hard but gives me a great sense of achievement.

On the days when Ephraim comes to pick me up from work after he finishes work himself, he meets the older children at the home, who follow me around and come along to see him. They call him Uncle Ephraim. When he arrives he usually hands them colorful candy and throws them high into the air, while they scream with terror and pleasure.

We go together to see Hannah and my other friends. It's the little time we have to be together, to hug with warmth and passion that lead to seductive, intimate kisses that leave us breathless and stop us from feeling the cold, the wind, or the rain.

* * * *

We arrive at Beit Hahalutzot with flushed faces and frozen hands. February is on its way. It's so cold that it might even snow in Tel Aviv. The weather prevents us from going out and Ephraim brings a newspaper in Hebrew with him. It includes the dots and lines under the letters that represent the vowels in Hebrew. I still haven't gotten used to the fact that vowels in Hebrew aren't represented by letters. He reads us excerpts and I learn about the events of the day. We pass the time talking about today's news and the topic of main concern to us is the ongoing debate in the Knesset on negotiating with Germany on a reparations agreement for the victims of the Nazis.

Angrily, I argue, "It's not up to the members of the Knesset to decide whether or not to accept compensation. It's our opinion that should count as the survivors. If I receive compensation, I'll be able to complete my education, which ended sometime in elementary school. Money can't compensate us for the loss of our families, but it can improve our future."

I'm surprised by how strong an impression my statement makes on the others. Out of the corner of my eye, I can see how proud of me Ephraim is that I gave my little speech and I feel that I can escape my narrow world. There are new times ahead for me.

* * * *

I was born in February, and I'll be nineteen years old in a few days' time. It's not even a year since I came to Israel, and there have been so many changes in my life.

On my birthday, Ephraim comes to pick me up from work and hands me a small, giftwrapped box, but not before showering me with frenzied kisses that make me dizzy.

I open the box and find a gold chain with a Star of David. I turn pale, freeze on the spot, and lower my head. I don't utter a word. I'm afraid of his reaction. He's leaving me no choice but to reveal that I'm hiding the Rita from him who has faith, but who prays to Mother Mary before bed and wears a cross around her neck.

Ephraim lifts my head and looks at me in amusement. "My sweet Rita," he says. "You're clever but still very naïve. What do you think? That I don't know about the cross you wore the day we went to Suzy, the day when you asked me to love you and I touched your breasts? Do you think I didn't feel the cross that you were wearing?"

My white face blushes and turns a fiery red. Again, the man I'm in love with is making fun of me.

Ephraim bursts out laughing at the sight of my hot face and states, "Since the day you asked me to love you without knowing how much I was already in love with you, you've always made sure to take off your cross whenever we meet. I don't know if you stopped wearing it entirely and if you still pray to Mother Mary, and I don't care. Not at all. I also don't care if under your blouse you wear both a cross and a Star of David together. Or even if you add a Buddha. I wouldn't be particularly happy if you also add Muhammad, but even that's an option. You know I'm entirely secular."

I'm confused when he puts the necklace around my neck and says seriously, "But...I do have one request: that you wear this necklace with the Star of David on our wedding day."

Stunned, I burst out laughing and say, "You must be joking. You're not serious, are you?"

"Yes I'm serious, I mean every word I said."

After I calm down I answer, "What an original way to propose." My heart is exploding with happiness, but I give him back as good as he gives. "I'm very young, you know, I'll have to think about your proposal."

We're holding hands when we return to Beit Hahalutzot. We're both deep in thought, and from time to time, Ephraim sneaks a worried look at me. I find it flattering, and I say to myself, I may be naïve but I learn quickly from you. I'm a good student.

The newspaper says that snow is expected in Tel Aviv as well. Some say it hasn't happened in over a century.

Chapter 45

Even though my heart is filled with joy and the desire to say, "Yes, yes, I will," I wait a while before giving Ephraim an answer to his indirect marriage proposal. I find myself enjoying the feeling of power that comes with leaving him waiting in expectation after our beginning and I begged for his love in my innocent way without realizing that his actions indicated how he felt. In his wisdom, Ephraim doesn't press me, and I can't hold out any longer. In the end I can't wait and I declare, "Yes, I want to."

I am once again little Rita trapped in my love for him. I'm thrilled. I can't stop smiling. For the first time since I can remember, I have nothing to hide. All traces of anxiety have disappeared. Good days are coming my way.

* * * *

Our wedding will be held in a month, in the middle of March. The weather is improving, the sun and the wind are drying the benches in Meir Park by the residence. We take advantage of the clear days to sit on our favorite bench, which is hidden from passersby under the dense and thick branches of a sycamore tree.

I surrender to Ephraim's arms and tell him, "You know Ephraim, sometimes I thank Uncle Moshe for bringing me here. I feel like I it's where I belong, and I finally have the document that proves I exist. My Israeli identity card is a source of security for me, it gives me a sense of belonging. Israel is my country and this is where I'll raise our children. And I want a big family. I remember, or maybe I just think I do, that when I stepped off the ship, despite being angry at Uncle Moshe's deception, I felt like this is where I'm welcome."

Moved by my words, Ephraim hugs me tightly and whispers softly in my ear, "What would have happened if you hadn't gone on that trip to Paris with Uncle Moshe, if you'd become nuns—would you be happy?"

"As for Suzy, the answer is clear. But as for me, maybe. Maybe if I'd joined a convent in Africa." After a few seconds of silence, I add, "The truth is, I'm not entirely sure that I would have been happy as a nun in Africa. I'm not entirely sure because from time to time I would find myself longing for a family of my own. I always remembered my father's words when he said goodbye to me on the day he took us to the convent: 'Don't forget that you're Jewish.' I also remember what the Mother Superior said to me: 'Rita, you belong to the Jewish people who lost so many of their sons and daughters.' When we refused to see Uncle Moshe, she told us that family is very important. I truly appreciate the wisdom of that woman. She was like a mother to me. I'm so sad that Papa won't be at our wedding. It hurts that he won't meet you." Tears wet my cheeks.

* * * *

We spend our last Saturday evening before the day of the wedding at Meir Park, which I look at every morning from my window. I can smell that spring is on the way, and the longing in my body, which follows. In the darkness of evening, we experience wonderful moments. We don't feel the time passing as our bodies are carried away in passion, but still not beyond the limit I set.

Ephraim has trouble understanding. "After all, we are about to get married!"

I stick to my guns. Something inside me orders me to stop, not to break the taboo in my education.

"Patience, Ephraim, wait with patience, conquer your desire until our wedding day. It's a holy day. I feel the same as you, I'm also exhausted by the need to control myself, but there's a voice dissuading me and telling me to wait."

"Have you noticed, Rita, my nun, that the word wait sounds the same as weight. Waiting is like a heavy weight. Sometimes I imagine you as the bud of a wonderful blooming rose, and its petals are opening up to me a little more each time, but too slowly...and the stem has thorns."

His words fill me with pleasure and I reply with a giggle, "It's incredible, Ephraim, what the need to realize our love does to you. Not only are you strong enough to carry the weight, you're also being very expressive. I love your description of the beauty in waiting for more. You really have the soul of a poet," I add with a touch of cynicism.

Ephraim answers me, "Mock me, mock me, I hope you reach full bloom by our wedding day."

We make up with a long hug and kiss until the park guard kicks us out.

* * * *

Aunt Rachel comes with me to buy a wedding dress. I choose a simple dress because it's a gift from Uncle Dov and Aunt Rachel. Uncle Moshe is organizing and paying for the wedding. Is that all? I ask myself. I would have expected more substantial financial help from my uncles than a dress and a wedding. It makes me angry and reminds me of the wad of cash that Uncle Moshe gave to Uncle Dov when we were staying with him, and what Gadi said about Uncle Moshe's job, traveling around the world and raising money to bring orphaned Jewish children to Israel. I link the two, and construct an unflattering explanation for their behavior. I share my anger with Ephraim and he admits that he's also disappointed, and he insists on paying for the wedding buffet himself.

He then tries to make my theory easier to swallow and explains, "Perhaps they're acting this way because they're disappointed that I'm not religious, and as for you, they're not sure what you believe. You have another reason to be angry with your uncles, which I didn't tell you before because I wanted to spare you. Your Uncle Moshe took advantage of your belief and your poor knowledge of geography. Instead of taking you home from Paris by train and traveling north to Antwerp, he drove you south to the port of Marseille. This, on the grounds that returning by sea would add something to the trip. This in itself was deceiving, because to return from Marseille to Antwerp by sea, you have to go through the Strait of Gibraltar, the Atlantic Sea, and the English Channel. It's a very long way."

I'm embarrassed but after thinking for a moment, I answer with a smile, "That's true, we were naive and ignorant. But if I'd understood his cunning intention and refused to go, I wouldn't have met you."

To this, Ephraim answers, "There's a saying, 'a blessing in disguise.'"

And I add, "A blessing for us both."

* * * *

Today, when Ephraim comes to pick me up from work and take me to my residence, he announces, "There's a change of plans. Today, we're going to look for an apartment to rent. I looked into the matter. They're building a new neighborhood near Tel Aviv called Ramat Gan."

We're greeted by a row of small two-story buildings surrounded by endless white sands, which we sink into. The roads and sidewalks are yet to be paved. Practical as usual, Ephraim leaves the dreams to me but I quickly return to gray reality and ask anxiously where the money will come from.

"From both of our salaries. I'm finishing my bookkeeping course, so my salary will increase considerably, and I have savings we can use. I have the plans for a two-room apartment we can afford. I have a copy for you too. You can choose the furniture and equipment we need and decorate it as you like."

Hand in hand, we wander through the stores. Simple furniture inhabits our nest, which is where we'll go after the wedding. Sometimes Ephraim's sister, Hannah, joins us. I grin widely with pleasure during these family togetherness times.

* * * *

Tomorrow's our wedding day, and today we're forbidden to see each other until the huppah is held. It makes no sense to me. In fact, I find it upsetting. The wedding ceremony and everything it involves is not to my liking. I'm led under the canopy by Aunt Hela, and Ephraim is led by Uncle Moshe. I anxiously touch my neck to see if I forgot to wear the Star of David. I relax, it's in place.

The canopy is on one side of the synagogue hall, and on the opposite wall there are two tables with light refreshments. Chairs for the guests are arranged on both sides of the aisle leading to the canopy. One side is for the men, while the other is for the women. Church is much more beautiful than the synagogue, with its bare walls. The church's walls are decorated with stunning stained glass windows and the guests aren't separated into men and women, especially when celebrating a union between a man and a woman.

Through the veil covering my face, I can barely recognize my own guests, who are engulfed in the sea of Uncle Moshe's religious guests...men with beards and women wearing headscarves. I'm led round and round Ephraim until my head spins and I don't remember the exact order of the ceremony. When Ephraim puts the ring on my finger, I wait for my turn to put a ring on his, but it turns out that it's not customary in a Jewish wedding, only among Christians. Disappointed by the ring matter, I'm startled by the sound of the glass breaking and the sudden loud mazal tovs.

By the end of the ceremony, after the speeches are made, some of which I don't understand, my feet are aching in my new shoes that are as white as the dress. I'm surrounded on all sides by guests, most of whom I don't know. Out of the corner of my eye I catch Uncle Moshe's happy face. He's also surrounded by guests. He's truly happy because he's saved a Jewish soul, and I soften and forgive him because it was due to him that I met Ephraim.

For a few seconds, his face changes into Papa, who smiles at me and says, "Thank you for not forgetting what I asked of you on the day I left you at the convent: to remember that you're Jewish, and to find a Jewish husband. You've given me and Mama great happiness."

Uncle Moshe's religious guests congratulate us. "Mazal tov, congratulations, what a privilege it is for you that such distinguished guests are attending your wedding, and that the chief rabbi of Tel Aviv himself married you."

I whisper into Ephraim's ear, "The real privilege is that we found each other after such different paths in life, because we have the same roots."

And Ephraim whispers back to me, "And from these roots, we'll bring up a warm family and children firmly rooted in this land and sure of their identity."

Printed in Great Britain
by Amazon